VISITING

Previous publications by The Uni Writers:

The Channel Collection (2012)

VISITING

A COLLECTION OF POEMS & STORIES

The Uni Writers

Printed by imprintdigital
Upton Pyne, Exeter
www.imprintdigital.net

Typeset by narrator
www.narrator.me.uk
enquiries@narrator.me.uk

Published by The Uni Writers
Channel House, The Channel, Ashbourne, Derbyshire, DE6 1FB

First published 2013

ISBN: 978 0 9927858 0 2

CONTENTS

INTRODUCTION

Visiting is a wonderful anthology. Firstly and foremost is the way the writing brings the world alive. All the writers here have a knack for finding the telling detail, the interesting angle, as well as for asking big questions and exploring life in all its richness, difficulty and wonder. But the key to the book is in many ways its title. The book is themed around *Visiting*, and reading these pages is like going on a journey around the world, with flashbacks and memories of the landscapes, people and familiarity of home. We are taken to places as exotic, interesting and as far-flung as Sierra Leone, Delhi, Argentina, Cambodia, and elsewhere, returning at various points to Ashbourne, Chatsworth, Lowry, Simon Manby's Studio, and to the dramas, worries and joys of real and ordinary lives at home.

But this anthology travels in other ways too. It is deliberately restless, varied and full of surprises, and delightfully free-spirited in its exploration of both subjects and styles. We find stories, travel writing, essays, meditations, flash fictions, memory pieces, as well as experimental, free verse and rhyming poetry. I'm tempted to suggest that this book could help to reduce climate change, as we can sit on our sofas at home, and travel the world – without having to worry about baggage allowances or currency conversion!

With the careful evocation of place at its centre, and with wonderful range of tone and effect, this book is a generous feast, of blacksmiths, babies, aliens, love, rifles, birds, children, theatre, war, Joseph Wright, Rapunzel – and I haven't even really begun.

Read on, stay at home, enjoy and explore the world at leisure…

Matt Black

Award-winning poet and
Derbyshire poet laureate (2011-2013)

Visiting

THE HOME

Peter Breheny

The man had made a habit of visiting his mother and father when he needed guidance to overcome problems in his life. His visits gave him the opportunity to see them at regular intervals and he was happy to see them in such good health. Since he'd been visiting them in this place they had regained their old vigour and love of life. Here everything was perfect, they had no worries and they'd made new friends. Many of their friends were famous people and the man was always surprised to see how well his parents mixed with people who in their time had been people of international stature.

As he entered the room, tired from his journey and half asleep, his mother waved to him from a table where she was surrounded by happy, laughing people, all taking tea. She beckoned for him to join her. She was surrounded by people he recognised from his childhood. Mrs Metzker, Mrs Golden, Mr Solomon and in the far corner of the room he recognised his grandparents deep in conversation with Rabbi Samuels.

'Come and sit, meet my new friend.' To his surprise the man sitting with his mother was a smiling Adolf Hitler – the man was speechless and horrified that his mother had befriended such a man. 'Shake hands with Adolf,' she said, 'we have become very good friends and I want that you should meet him.' Adolf winked at her and in response she touched him affectionately on the hand.

The man felt his blood pressure rise to boiling point – as the shock of who his mother had befriended registered with him. 'Mother, are you crazy? Don't you realise who this is?' 'Oh, don't be making such a fuss. Shake hands with Adolf and say hello.' Adolf smiled serenely and offered his hand in friendship. The man pulled back his own hand, disgusted and flabbergasted at his mother's suggestion. 'Mother, the man is a mass murderer, he killed members of your own family and millions of others and you want me to shake his hand?'

The man wanted to kill his mother's new friend – there and then. He felt it his duty to kill him, to kill him in the most painful way. He knew this opportunity would never present itself again but something inside him told him that in this place – it was everyone's right to be forgiven.

The man's mother smiled. 'Sit down son, you must learn to forgive and forget. Remember there is good in everyone – don't go looking for the worst in people all the time. You mustn't believe everything you're told – the Queen Mother was a bigger tyrant. I know. I met her.'

The man felt himself flying through time and space as the vision of his mother withered, lost somewhere deep inside his mind as he woke.

THE VISITOR

Nathanael Ravenlock

When I cry out in the night the visitor comes.

I open my eyes. The visitor is there standing over me. Large elliptical eyes stare down at me glittering in the twilight gathered room. I hold the visitor's gaze, trying to resist the control those eyes have over me. But my will falters. My eyelids grow heavy. The vision of the visitor blurs and I feel sleep flood my head.

I wake and cry out once more and the visitor comes.

My eyes open. The visitor is bathed in a cold thin blue light. The lips of the visitor part slightly and there comes a smooth hissing sound. I rock my head back and forth, throw my hands to my ears, try and banish that deep supernatural hum. But it penetrates my skull. Sinks into my mind. Its hypnotic tones massage my consciousness. A haziness flows through my body. My hands drop to my side. My muscles relax. My head lolls. I drift back to slumber.

I cry out and again the visitor comes.

Before I open my eyes I feel the visitor's presence. As I open my eyes the visitor slips a hand to my chest. My rib cage rises and falls rapidly as I try to take in air. The pressure of the visitor's hand waxes and wanes. Through the contact I feel the pulse of the visitor's blood as it swims through that mysterious hand. The rhythm of that pulse seeps into my body and soothes the rush of my blood. My heart rate slows. The visitor's pulse and mine dance in time. My breathing deepens. Each intake of air is measured under the steady beat of the visitor's heart. My soul slips towards the soft centre of sleep. My eyes close.

I do not cry out. I open my eyes cautiously. The visitor does not appear. The visitor has gone. I am sad. I am alone.

I speak to the darkness and the blue light appears. From the light comes the visitor and, as the visitor approaches, I smile. The visitor smiles back and lifts me to a soft embrace and we walk out of the darkness together.

THE HOST

Jo Manby

People visit the house, sometimes staying for an hour, sometimes for many decades at a time. They bring gifts, install possessions, and make objects, which, though ultimately transient, have their time as the building's chattels. Built around 1750 out of local sandstone, this was a forge in the heart of the village, where iron was worked, wrought into tools, wheel bonds or metal 'tyres', bolts, nails, horseshoes. People came to lean on the doorway, stand around the furnace, swap news, gossip, chew the fat.

I walk into the peaceful rooms downstairs around 7.30am in April. Where the forge entrance once stood, light filters through the salmon pink-lined coral-sprigged curtains to fill the pantry with its own pinkish dawn. Homemade marmalade glows like amber on the wooden shelf. Mineral accretions of orange zest the colour of fire caught in its substance, each jar named and dated like a museum artefact.

Where the blacksmith kept his charcoal are tins of Baxters soup; crystal dishes and glinting glassware; milky blue transfers on dimpling porcelain; wine glasses held aloft on their stems, airborne bubbles mounting the wall; scullery ornaments. Where there might have been awls, rasps, hammers, knives, there now lie a basket of fruit, a loaf defrosting on a plate for breakfast, Delftware serving dishes. A black casserole is the contemporary equivalent of the blacksmith's cast-iron household goods.

The pantry smells faintly of damp stone. The blacksmith was a farrier as well, making shoes for horses, knowledgeable about the anatomy of the horse's legs. The pungent, acrid scent of scorched horsehair and hooves would permeate the air for hundreds of yards around the forge, blending with the sonorous chime of hammer on anvil, the stamp and snort of the horses, the scrape of iron shoes on gravel, the sizzle of steam as red hot iron hit water. Now the pantry hums and rattles quietly with its fridge freezer.

As I stand in the pantry I try and sense the vestiges of industriousness. Before the invention of the bellows the blacksmith's apprentice would blow into the base of the hearth through hollow tubes. The 'man of fire' would carburise iron, repeatedly heating it up, quenching and hammering it and reheating it. The iron would thus be alloyed with more carbon and would be more elastic and tough – easier to work and with the capacity to sharpen to a fine blade. There would have been jokes, one-liners people shared around the entrance to the forge; children kicking stones, paddling in the brook; dogs sniffing around; hawkers and Romanies passing by.

In a blizzard, a traveller whose horse had lost a shoe on the journey would stop to have a new one made. The blacksmith would have had a way with horses that would calm them to stillness as he worked. In the eighteenth century, the philosopher Jean-Jacques Rousseau stayed in the village and I always imagined him walking past the place dressed in his Armenian costume of dark velvet, on his way back from the hills with pocketfuls of botanical specimens. In a village a blacksmith could also be a veterinary surgeon, a horse-dealer, an undertaker.

Now dried pink and beige hydrangeas hang on a string; tomatoes rest on a plate under Clingfilm. The iron hooks in the living room ceiling, originally for hanging flitches of bacon, would have been made by the blacksmith. He would be surrounded by his tools and equipment. Where there are blue and white striped jars, houseplants, stacks of gilded plates and bowls and dishes and a matching tureen, a pile of patty-pans, would have been his swage block, perforated with holes and with grooves down the sides, for heading bolts and nails and working iron pieces on; his moulds for casting popular household items such as flat irons and fire irons; his chisels, tongs, fullers, sledge hammers and bellows.

Now, objects with potential power are a primus stove and a kettle with a whistle for power cuts, a selection of torches, and the two automata – a rabbit that taps on a drum and a bird that bobs and sings – kept to entertain young children on rainy days. It is a place where provisions can be laid in for special celebrations, where hot jam can cool, where vegetables can keep: potatoes in the loamy darkness of their paper sack; apples stored divided into single layers; mushrooms from the fields and damsons from the orchard. There is a toast rack, a sauce boat, a cut-glass sweet dish; brandy, whisky, sloe gin.

In another room in the house at another time I have felt a breath on the back of my neck as I stood with my back to the table, as if someone had walked across the room empty of furniture and left their breath behind, hovering in the centre of the room. One winter, downstairs at five-thirty in the morning, I pulled back the curtains to look out and recoiled, quickly drawing them shut again; I thought I saw a gnarled grey face, or an old ram with a curled horn flat to its head. But there was no field for a sheep to stand on out there at that height anymore. The field had been dug away to make a drive a metre or so below the original level, some decades before.

Whispers and rumours about what went on in the shadowy forge after dark would circulate. In Medieval times some people thought the blacksmith was a magician; some were even burned as witches and blacksmithing banned at certain times and in certain places. Between its time as the forge and the gallery and studio that is the current line of business the place had been a farm. Where we lived and walked and sat and read and ate, cattle had been kept, butter churned, curds turned into cheese and straw strewn on earth floors.

Elisions of footsteps, imbrications of voices that have been and gone slide into a state of elusiveness. When our Dad used to carve his sculptures, before he turned to bronze as his main medium, the village centre again rang out with the sound of hammering. Not iron on iron but iron on stone, shaping new objects the exact like of which had not existed before. He sometimes referred to Michelangelo's theory that each stone contained a sculpture that the sculptor had then to extract. Similarly one has to be in the quiet rooms downstairs very early in the morning to sense the presence of the visitors. Those who have stayed briefly, those who lived there over the centuries, as if the house that was once a farm, and before that a forge, harbours traces of their lives within its stony walls.

THE VISITORS

Patricia Ashman

In her ground floor flat, Agnes Mary was terrified.

She had looked out at the front a few minutes earlier and seen the two men in dark uniforms stop and stare up at the front door.

Now she sat gripping the arms of her chair, unable to move. She stared at her door, at the bolts and complicated locks and the spy hole which the nice policeman had assured her would keep her safe.

She knew that every window was fast shut as they had been for the last three months since… since… no, she couldn't even think about it. The French windows had been replaced with new double glazed, double locked patio doors. She had wanted them boarded over, but fire regulations would not allow it.

Outside, the garden, for which she was responsible, was a wilderness, all her beautiful plants long gone to seed and the lawn a three-foot-high jungle for local cats on the prowl.

Her eyes strayed to the sideboard drawer where the newspaper cuttings lay,

Widow, 83, tied up and beaten by bogus Water Board men

and she began to tremble.

***

Down in the basement, Carol, too, had seen the dark clad legs stop outside, and this had provoked frantic activity on her part. Placing little Julie on the bed, she had pushed the chest of drawers in front of the door, put the table upside down on top of it, followed by the two chairs and two boxes of books. It wasn't much, but perhaps if she kept very quiet…

She had been expecting this. Behind with the rent and the payments on the TV, microwave, fridge and furniture, she also owed £2,500 on her credit card and the supermarket had refused to take it last week.

Carol had been so sure that she could manage on her own, but she liked nice things and wanted Julie to have the toys and clothes that other little girls had. Now they must have come to take it all back.

Picking up the baby again, she slipped into the tiny bathroom and sat on the floor with her back against the closed door.

***

Marty Greaves was a gambler and proud of it – well, he used to be. A bit flash in his choice of suits, the lapels just a little too sharp, and positively flamboyant in the tie department.

He was no ordinary punter, oh no. The words mathematical genius always sprang into his mind when he devised a new system. He had had minor triumphs over the years in various European casinos, even been banned from Monte once, but in recent years successes had been few and far between.

Which was why he presently resided in this sparsely furnished first floor flat in a run-down part of a strange town.

He had money, oh yes, lots of it, but the acquiring of it had been, he had to admit, not in his usual style. He had used his genius, and it had taken lots of brain work, but, in short, he had cheated.

All casino owners were totally devoid of pity, and Franco, the one he'd taken for a ride, was a ruthless bastard with friends on both sides of the law.

Now he'd sent his heavies to collect, for what else could they be, those two men he'd seen from his bay window? Youngish, broad shouldered and wearing those rather theatrical dark suits, he'd bet ten to one they'd got dark glasses in their top pockets.

Well, he'd rehearsed this moment. He slid the small case out from under the bed. No need to check it, he'd done that a dozen times. New passport, change of clothes, toilet bag and the letters which identified him as the holder of the off-shore account in the country for which he was heading.

The bedroom window, which he'd kept greased with Vaseline, opened smoothly. He tossed out the rope ladder secured to hooks under the window sill and then threw the suitcase down.

"Raffles, that's me", he thought as he lowered himself over the edge.

Before the two men began to mount the steps up to the front door, Marty was over the garden wall and away.

***

Shelly was fourteen years old, but she looked anything from eighteen to twenty-two.

Full figure, watchful knowing eyes, she had easily fooled the agent when she rented this tiny room tucked under the roof. He'd only been interested in the two months rent in advance, and when she paid in cash, he was satisfied.

Now, four months later, she had allowed a little hope to creep into her life. True, the money was going very fast, and she had only been able to find a job washing up in a greasy café, no questions asked, cash in hand, but she'd find something else soon.

She wished now that she'd taken more. A little planning and patience and she would have had five thousand, not just three, but she'd had to get away that very day. She could have taken a car too – she knew how to drive – but that would have been easy to trace.

Her dad was a used-car dealer. She had been eight years old when her mother died. It had only been six weeks before he had come to her bed and said that they should comfort each other.

She had not known what was happening, but it was painful, and she was frightened. Over the years she had come to feel deeply ashamed, too ashamed to ever speak to anyone about his regular use of her, and of course he warned her about what would happen to her if she did.

On her fourteenth birthday, she made her decision. She watched and waited for the right moment. He regularly had rolls of notes stuffed into the top drawer of his desk. His kind of business wasn't run with cheques and credit cards.

Then one day she overheard him talking to a friend of his, a fat, hairy scrap dealer whose glances always made her skin crawl.

They were watching her as she bent over washing a car.

"I'll lend her to you if you like – for a small fee," and they both laughed.

She knew that he didn't mean the car and that this was the day, ready or not, that she must go. That night, she took all the cash in the drawer, emptied the books out of her school bag and packed her few possessions.

Fifty pounds had been worth it to get her right away on three buses to a town she didn't know.

Now he'd found her. What else could those two men down there be, if not private detectives? They would drag her back to him. She was under age. He was her father.

***

As the knock came at the door, Agnes Mary felt the hot liquid seep through her clothes and into the chair as the acrid smell of urine filled the air. She let out one shuddering sob and tears began to roll down her wrinkled cheeks.

***

Carol clutched Julie so tightly that the child cried out.

"Sorry, sweetheart. Shush, Mummy's here".

She closed her eyes and prayed, something she hadn't done for years.

"Please God, don't let them take my baby".

***

In the ensuing silence, one of the young men on the doorstep turned to the other and said, "Well, brother, I don't think anyone here is interested in hearing about Jesus today. Let's try the next one".

At that very moment, Shelley jumped from the attic window.

ROUGH JUSTICE

Janis Clark

'Edna! You've come to arrest Edna!' Alan spluttered.

Edna said nothing.

'We have reason to believe…' began DC Barnes.

'Preposterous' shouted Alan.

Still Edna said nothing.

The twins looked from face to face, not sure whether this was exciting or something to worry about. Alan made an attempt to sound calm and told the boys to go to their rooms.

'Now what on *earth* are you saying?' he said turning to Barnes.

'Your mother in law is suspected of pushing your wife down the stairs,' said the detective patiently.

Alan almost laughed. 'For goodness sake man, she's in a *wheel*chair,' he said, stressing the wheel as if the detective was a simpleton.

'Just because someone's in a wheelchair, it doesn't mean…' explained the DC.

'She can't even get out of her room,' interrupted Alan angrily.

Edna lowered her head at this.

'We've had a comprehensive report from forensics,' began Barnes, 'and Mrs Redfern is believed to be implicated. We need her to come to the station for further questioning.'

At this point, both men turned to Edna who had her best child-like and wondering face on.

'Ooh!' she said. 'Are we going on a train? How lovely.'

They ignored her and returned to their quibbling.

'Look,' said Alan, 'could we just step in to the other room?' The detective nodded. The old lady was hardly likely to get up and run away.

Alan turned to her. 'Just going to make a cuppa, Edna.'

She nodded and smiled and the two men left her.

Edna dropped her smile and thought of Heather lying dead at the bottom of the stairs. Her body was funnily arranged, she'd thought. Her nightdress was up exposing her lower half but one leg had fallen in such a way as to hide her modesty.

Heather had replaced the lovely Sophie, Edna's only child, when Sophie had died in a car accident. Edna's eyes watered slightly at the memory.

She pictured Heather again in that undignified position and saw once more, the face, so often puckered in anger or lip-pursed in sarcasm or disapproval, that cruel smile of contempt saved for Edna and the boys whenever Alan was not there. As she lay, so obviously dead, with her twisted neck turning her face upwards, her eyes blank, Edna had thought, 'She's actually quite beautiful. What a shame!' and allowed herself only the merest hint of a smile.

THE VISIT

Vikki Fitt

Henry and I lock loving eyes across the breakfast table. My Tetley teabag drips over the edge of the Lowry teabag tidy (artfully designed in the shape of a teapot, with miniature mill scene; I can almost hear the artist rotating in his Mancunian grave). The long June day stretches endlessly before us. Just the two of us, in love, whiling away the hours till nightfall.

Henry's gaze intensifies. His eyes, fixed on mine, bulge meaningfully; his elfin face is transformed into a magenta balloon. No mistaking it: Henry is producing the first of today's mega-poos, and this before his parents have even disappeared over the brow of the hill to join the bustling ranks of London commuters.

I release him from his high-chair, struggling to avoid being grabbed by yoghurty fingers, and make a desperate stab at scrubbing the Farrow-and-Balled white walls, newly pebble-dashed with soggy Weetabix. Henry knows that a spoon (in his case, one gripped in each slimy paw) is involved in transferring food from dish to stomach, but hasn't yet mastered the skill of involving his mouth in the process, so that the food whizzes past his fuzzy head onto the nearest solid surface. The frustration that results from this means his hands delve into the depths of his cereal bowl and are then slapped against his scalp, running his fingers through his blond wisps like a tortured artist searching for inspiration.

Released from his prison, Henry crawls into the sitting-room, raising his hands carefully like a polar bear; this is a new skill. His compost-laden Pamper drags behind him like the abdomen of a wasp. He laboriously hauls himself up to a standing position, turns to smirk triumphantly at me and immediately loses his precarious balance, managing to lacerate his delicate cheek on the log basket as he plummets to the floor. The resulting screams will rouse the dozing denizens of Riverside Road. Oh God, it's not even 7.30am yet.

Calm is restored; a clean bottom, a quick fix of C-Beebies and Granny writhing on the carpet making enthusiastic animal noises whilst singing Old MacDonald on a loop have brought an illusion of peace. Nap time – I'm as ready for 40 winks as Henry is, coddled in his Grobag with Rabbit, the picture of contentment. I, on the other hand, am a whirling dervish of domestic activity, processing laundry and washing dishes with one febrile hand whilst preparing a three-course gourmet luncheon for his lordship with the other. He wakes. He has a cold. How can that have happened? He was the picture of health an hour ago. Now it's wall-to-wall snot, projectile sneezing and a temperature so high we could heat up the aforementioned (and now spurned) banquet on his burning forehead.

To the park. As we approach, Henry bounces with feverish (literally) anticipation as he spots his personal Holy Grail, the baby swings. He giggles and gurgles for a blissful half-hour till my arthritic joints scream for a rest from pushing. To divert Henry and counter his withdrawal symptoms, we head to the lake where flocks of swans and assorted duck families are strutting their stuff and gobbling hunks of unnutritious white bread thrown by eager toddlers. We park up at a bench by the water's edge. Sucking a breadstick, Henry is in seventh heaven.

"Look at the lovely swan, Henry!" I coo as a huge beast sidles up to us. Goodness, he's enormous close up, with a beak like a mechanical steel trap and malicious beady eyes. Those psychopathic eyes are fixed on my innocent grandson, blissfully unaware of approaching danger, or rather are fixed on his semi-macerated breadstick. Fleeting images flash through my mind of explaining 'The Attack' to his parents, as the baby lies bandaged like the Invisible Man in A and E. Then my panic-stricken brain slips into reptilian mode, I leap to my feet and jump in a star shape at the swan whilst shrieking "BOO!"; I have been told this is the way to deal with grumpy bullocks should you find yourself on the receiving end of their hormonal attacks. The swan rears and launches itself at me with a malevolent hiss but my protective dander is up.

"Come on, make my day!" I spit back as I seize the Bugaboo controls and run like hell for the sanctuary of the cathedral cloisters. Never again will we feed the ducks without full body armour and visors. We might look foolish but, then again, we'd be unrecognisable – and safe.

6pm and the parental cavalry arrives, my son-in-law bringing me a medicinal balloon glass filled with Sauvignon Blanc as Henry and I lie in a semi-comatose embrace on the lawn, both stupefied with fatigue. It's a toss-up as to which of us will hit the sack first...

THE TORTOISES' PICNIC

Annie Noble

I came across "The Tortoises' Picnic" in a book; a collection chosen by Michael Rosen entitled, *Funny Stories*, re-published by Kingfisher in 2005. It's a delightfully eclectic mix of original stories by various authors as well as folk tales from different countries which have been kept close to their original form, and of folk tales that Michael Rosen has re-written. The Tortoises' Picnic is billed as an English Folk Tale. This in itself pleased me because it is such a silly story and where did it first originate? Because it certainly wasn't back in the long-ago days when we English sat around our firesides in the darkness and quiet after a day's work was done, telling stories! You will see why when you read the poem!

I have taken some liberties with the story in re- setting it in my local landscape for the delectation of a poetry group I belong to in the village. So Paradise Pool is a family name for a favourite place in the woods and other names are accurate and can be found on the map. I wrote it in a spirit of joy when many weeks of wet weather had finally been routed by a high pressure system bringing SUNSHINE!

The Tortoises' Picnic

At the top of the churchyard, underneath the yew,
Lived Mummy Tortoise, Daddy Tortoise and Little Tortoise too.
One day, as he lay dreaming of lettuce and of grass
He heard his mother shouting, "The sun has come at last!"

Little Tortoise stretched his head from underneath his shell,
To see this wondrous object of which he had heard tell.
In its bright glare he winked and blinked, then giggled in the heat.
The only thing he knew about was having four wet feet!

His mother lay there sunbathing, spread-eagled on her back.
His father looked embarrassed and gave his son a thwack.
"Come on my lad, and Mother! The time has come at last
When we can go and picnic beneath this fiery blast."

"I know the spot exactly where we will dine in bliss.
The opportunity is one that is far too good to miss.
We'll pack the bags with goodies such as you have never seen.
We'll steal them from the vicar – he'll not know we've been!"

Mummy Tortoise and Little Tortoise shouted with delight,
"Oh, where is it we're going? Will we be there by night?"
Daddy Tortoise smiled and said, "That's not for me to say,
For we'll have to walk a while and it is a long, long way."

The place that we are going is known as Paradise Pool,
After walking in this summer heat it will be very cool.
Those endless days of rain are over, of that I am quite sure
There are many days of sunshine to warm us to the core."

They trundled off to find their food, all groaning with delight,
At the thought of cake and sandwiches, of beer and squash and Sprite.
Inside the vicar's larder they filled their bags with grub.
By the time that they had finished they could have stocked a pub!

There were all the things they'd thought of – of others only dreamt.
That great big tin of honeyed ham must have been heaven-sent.
"It's the crowning glory," Daddy Tortoise said, "Of this feast we plan to eat.
How fortunate it really is there's tin around the meat!"

"For that will keep our tummies safe from germs, those nasty, horrid things,
And therefore we will dine right well on a banquet fit for kings."
Mummy Tortoise nodded with a happy smile upon her face,
And Little Tortoise ran in circles at a very fearsome pace.

With grass they tied their bulging bags upon their shelly backs,
Then swiftly, ere the vicar's return, they bent their stealthy tracks.
They plodded through the grasses and climbed a wall or two
Before night-time came upon them and the grass was wet with dew.

They stopped to slumber at the bus stop, beneath a wooden seat
Before a rude arousing by a boy with great big feet.
Again they plodded onwards in the rising rays of sun
Keeping right on walking until the day was done.

Their legs were getting weary and their feet were hurting too.
Though Little Tortoise trundled on, his mood was getting blue.
But the family motto, it was inscribed upon each shell.
"A job that once is started – it must be done right well!"

It was the last day of July when first they trundled forth,
Three times the sun had been and gone by Honeywall Lane North.
With empty tums and blistered feet they limped on down the hill,
Past Potters farm and onwards until they reached the cattle grill.

Up the hill, past Mottcarn Barn, was where their path did lead,
Then, beneath the gate, downhill, through grass where they did feed.
Just a little mouthful was all that Daddy Tortoise let them munch
To make sure they would not spoil their delightful picnic lunch.

They crept beneath the fence into Ordley Woods dank shade,
And fought through bracken tall and tangled, hoping for a glade
Where they could rest and gird their loins and have a little doze,
Before they reached that dappled pool, where they could cool
their toes.

Fourteen days had come and gone and still the days were hot,
When finally Daddy Tortoise shouted, "Oh, joy is now our lot!
Another day should see us in that longed-for picnic site,
How we shall enjoy ourselves when that ham does see the light!"

The family groaned with hunger and fought through nettles tall,
They were bounced upon by rabbits and hit once by a ball.
But finally the moment came for which they all did long,
Their eyes beheld the dappled pool and they broke out in song.

The brook flowed right smoothly o'er a rocky bit of shelf,
Into the brown and dappled depths of Paradise Pool itself.
A fish finned through the water to hide in shadows dark,
And a blackbird trilled his story as sweetly as a lark.

Their tiredness gone, those tortoises, they made their way pell mell,
To reach the longed-for heaven of that dingly, cool dell.
They laid their bags upon the shingle and paddled in the stream.
At last they'd reached fulfilment of their happy dream.

Mummy Tortoise spread the rug, unpacked the bags of food.
The sight of that provender put them all in jolly mood!
With tummies rumbling loudly and dribbling with delight,
Daddy Tortoise and Little Tortoise prepared to take a bite.

But even as their mouths did open, Mummy Tortoise shouted crossly,
"No, no I say! You've got to stop! You cannot eat your tea!
For something is forgotten and we really must not start
Until the ham is opened, else it will break my heart. . ."

Tears dripped fast as she spoke these words, then hid within her shell.
Daddy Tortoise looked askance and shouted, "Tell, oh tell!
My dear, my darling what is wrong? Why do you weep and sob?
The tin opener is all we need to do a right good job."

Mummy Tortoise sniffed and said, "That's exactly what I mean.
The tin opener is absolutely nowhere to be seen.
We must have left it far behind, underneath the yew,
Or perhaps it lies forgotten, rusting in a pew."

She stuck her head from neath her shell and looked at Little Tortoise.
"It must be your fault it is forgotten," she said with voice quite raucous.
"So you must go and get it, proceed at once, I say,
Dad and I will wait right here whilst you do make your way."

Little Tortoise scowled and said, "I don't see why I should.
By the time I return with it you will have eaten all the food.
"Oh no, Oh no," they both did cry, "We promise we will wait.
We'll hide the food quite safely and then we'll hibernate."

So Little Tortoise trundled off and his parents kept their promise.
They packed the food and concealed it, then parting with a kiss
They said good night and slumbered, for days and nights together,
Until they finally woke up and found a change in weather.

The leaves had fallen from the trees and on the ground was frost.
Of Little Tortoise there was no sign. It seemed he must be lost.
"We must go home at once and find him," Mummy Tortoise cried,
"But before we go, I must have some of that good food inside."

Daddy Tortoise nodded and reached into the gloom,
Where the bags had long lain hidden in their earthy tomb.
He opened up the nearest one and handed to his wife,
A loaf of bread, some butter and the bent old kitchen knife.

She'd no sooner had a nibble of this delightful spread
Than they heard an angry shout from somewhere overhead.
The voice of Little Tortoise came yelling, loud and clear,
"I knew I couldn't trust you. I was filled with such dire fear,"

That you would start, as you have done, upon the picnic feast,
Oh, Mother dear, I really think that you are a horrid beast.
How fortunate I stayed here to keep an eye on you.
If the tin opener is needed – well, it's up to you two!"

VIEW FROM A REAR WINDOW

Harry Wilson

The view from the bay window of my favourite room in my Ashbourne home has a rear view, embracing a wide vista. This room, my snug, has walls festooned with pictures of my mountaineering successes, and faces east catching the morning sun. The view takes in a lawn, a circular pool and two-tier fountain, a summer house flanked by two white, well off-white, statues. Behind the lawn is a large orchard with fields beyond.

I spend most of my time in this room, especially in winter, reading and writing. Every morning the first two hours are spent reading my vouchered Times, cover to cover, and then, usually, I pick up one of my many books on Francis Drake… I am a founder member of The Francis Drake Society. When sitting at my ancient knee-hole desk, I gaze, thinking, out of the rear window, absorbing every detail.

The pool and fountain are a popular meeting place for a wide variety of wild birds. Often I see larger birds bullying the smaller varieties pushing them away. The other prominent features are the two near full size statues of Leonardo da Vinci's boy David, naked and unashamed, whose head is turned, looking longingly at the scantily clad, pale and wan Daphne who faces the other way.

Beyond the lawn is an old orchard of unpruned apple and pear trees, a bird's paradise especially in autumn when the grounded, unpicked fruit are a welcome bird food larder.

Suddenly, slowly streaking across the sky, mainly a.m., southbound, are vapour trails streaming from barely visible aeroplanes, which eventually fizzle out. In a matter of minutes many more trails appear on what must be a busy route. I imagine these jet planes flying from London or Paris destined for New York or Miami, all at heights well above that of Everest. I see hostesses in their chic tabards partially covering expensive designer uniforms, attending to passengers' every need and fielding a wide range of flight related questions.

Then, I see countless wild birds flying, some erratically, across the orchard heading nowhere in particular, parking high on tree tops, some loners, for a considerable length of time. With so many birds in the air, diving and circling, I am reminded of Heathrow holding patterns. I'm sure you have noticed birds have remarkable braking systems, full pelt to instant full stop. They must have 20/20 vision to see food, or predators, at speed. Just like jet planes, birds' flight variations must be related to power-to-weight ratios.

You know, I have never seen a dead wild bird! Do predators take them and dispose of their bodies? Or, are they like cats when they know they are dying they just slip away to hedge-bottoms? Which leads me to another question, is heaven exclusively for humans? When humans die their soul or spirit is said, by most religions, to ascend to a heavenly state. Do birds and animals have souls that find their way to the same spiritual home? Heaven by now must be mightily overcrowded.

A solo low-flying blackbird flies by seeking safety. In the far part of the orchard a male pheasant is making advances to a retreating female… cherchez la femme in this weather?! A numbing, freezing fog takes over and with it an eerie silence. Birds must have their own retreats to escape such weather conditions.

Early afternoon, the disorientating fog clears and normal bird activity resumes with conditions still icy. A cheeky robin wheels on to a bush immediately in front of the window, looks straight at me, tarries awhile then swoops off to find elusive larders. A sparrow hurriedly circumnavigates the paved edge of the ice-covered pool then heads off to the orchard. A squirrel, haltingly, makes it way along the top rung of the wooden fence separating lawn from orchard, jumps down and brazenly lollops to the next garden. I thought squirrels hibernated! Vapour trails appear. That evening the BBC forecasted more frost, ice and snow.

Sure enough, the following morning it was bitterly cold with sky completely covered with light and dark grey clouds. This, in aviation parlance, is termed eight oktas, representing the unit of measurement to record cloud cover. The trees in the orchard are stark and blackened with even the flimsiest branches – stock still. No larger birds were in flight with the odd tit flitting desperately for food on a berryless bush.

The following day the view from my window was a fairy-tale scene and brass monkey weather. Everywhere was covered in 8cms of snow. The silence was deafening. The horizon sky was in three distinct strata – light blue merging into dark blue with the foreground a light grey, a view to remember. Not a bird or squirrel dared to venture out no doubt keeping to the safety of hedges and perhaps even house eaves? Recalling a similar weather situation I decided to check the attic of my home. Pulling down the loft ladder, I was surprised to see a chorus line of BATS hanging upside down from a cross beam. As a protected species what could I do? I decided not to disturb the creatures hoping they would depart of their own volition as the weather improved… they did.

Suddenly, as if from nowhere, some 30 seagulls came swooping and diving into the orchard, their erratic flight lasted only a few minutes before, as quickly as they arrived, they left continuing, I suppose, their search for food. Normally, I see a lone seagull slowly gliding with minimal use of their wings. I recall last winter I saw an elegant heron casually drifting down on to the pool. Seeing it was fishless, it moved onto the pool next door which contained large goldfish but protected by netting – no luck there.

Shortly after, and equally as sudden after the departure of the seagulls, starlings by the score descended on to the orchard in a more orderly fashion. They swooped under the fruit trees where they knew they would find rich pickings. They scratted and hopped about in short breaks each trying to find places to forage… at times the scene was frantic. An hour or so later I witnessed their instantaneous departure as if their leader had blown a whistle.

This incident reminded me of a business trip to Melbourne, Australia when, invited to walk through a dense wood, I was startled by the loud sound of countless cricket insects – such noise was produced by the rubbing together of legs, a sort of high pitched grating. The sound was repeated at regular intervals and started and stopped in an instant together as if by a cricket conductor leading an orchestra. The intervals lasted about two minutes with the whole choir back in full voice. This unusual vibrative phenomenon lasted throughout the whole visit to the woods.

Today is an early January morning, sharp and bitingly cold. I quickly hopped out of bed, showered and dressed hastening breakfast before retiring to the sanctuary of my snug. Looking out, the first thing that catches my eye is the pale, light blue sky with clouds like streaky bacon seemingly motionless. Momentarily I stretch my mind thinking of deep outer space penetrating the mysteries of the universe to the finite end… do we then fall off the edge? With the shake of my head I come back down to earth.

Looking from my window across the orchard, through a tunnel of trees, to the far field, I caught a glimpse of a group of youths gathered around an old, much admired, chestnut tree. They were on private land so what were they up to? I went to investigate. On approach a few scattered but three or four remained. There was no hurling of abuse. They said they were building a tree house. They had a ladder from which they used roped to haul planks and the tree house was well advanced and looked safe enough. As they were not damaging the tree, I mildly remonstrated, advising they were trespassing and they could stay as long as they removed the tree house at the end of the school holiday. Their initiative therefore was approved and they did remove the construction.

Slap in the middle of the orchard is an old misshapen pear tree which, as a result of howling gales, is now leaning at an acute angle with roots protruding above ground. It is sad at any time to see a tree in such a helpless condition – almost like a ship blown on to rocks. Hanging from two frayed thick ropes is a rotting wooden seat still gently swinging. There is no carefree laughter of children shouting 'Higher, higher", or Dad, atop a ladder, gently directing pears into gaping hands. Gone are those sublime, al fresco days with children now married with children of their own who now play not in the orchard but on paved areas completely plasticated... swings, pedal cards, bouncing platforms etc., more fun perhaps but less joyous... oh, happier days!

Slowly the scene changes, stealthily, fog moves in right to left and birds just disappear.

THE CHRISTMAS VISIT

Denis Quigley

They walked briskly up the hill, tension circling them, the crunch of their steps on the icy snow taking the place of the angry words coiling at the backs of their tongues. He moved ahead, a combination of his longer legs and her lack of fitness. She struggled, panting, but letting the anger drive her onwards. Anger at his lack of sympathy, anger at her bad choices, anger at her sisters for their greed, anger at the mistake they'd made by coming. She crested the hill. He stood stiffly at the little monument, staring out over the snow-filled valley.

Far below, the water was a grey choppy mass, reflecting the toneless grey sky. At the far end there was a stand of firs, green at the edges fading quickly to a black mass. The trees that sprawled on the hillside and crowded the banks had lost their leaves, and the long grey branches twisted in the wind.

She stood beside him for a few moments and said, "It's not my fau.." but he swung round to face her and the words died on her tongue.

He breathed heavily for a moment, "No. It's not your fault, and its not my fault. So let's say nothing about it and just walk."

The path down to the lake was easy, the snow flattened by the boots and sledges of families working off their Christmas dinners, and even on Boxing Day the few icy sections had been gritted. He started off at a brisk pace then, realising she was falling behind again, relented and coming back wordlessly hooked his arm in hers. The path wove in and out of the trees. Though leafless they gave some protection from the wind and when they moved through the open sections she could feel him shiver. She went to commiserate, suggest they turn back, but at the thought of drawing attention to his cheap coat she heard her brother-in-law's loud, braying voice at the dinner table, "...had to buy us all new kit for the New Year skiing holiday. Cost me thousands but the kids insisted on designer gear and I wasn't going to let Molly and me suffer with the cold. Need to buy the best, old son." It wasn't that she envied them their money, well maybe a little bit, but did they have to go on and on about it when they knew he'd been made redundant?

His anger kept him warm and the icy touch of the wind on his face just made him feel more alive. As they entered the next stand of trees there was a fallen tree at the edge of the path. Snow had gathered along the trunk, deepening at the hollow where the remains of a great branch stuck out. On the trunk he could see the prints where some small mammal had run along then disappeared into a tiny snow burrow, perhaps a mouse or a shrew. A shrew he decided. Maybe it was one of the evil sisters in her night-time form. Well, maybe not evil but certainly vile, Anastasia and Drizella for sure.

The cost of petrol and the B&B had taken the last of the carefully hoarded balance on his credit card so she'd haunted the charity shops to find something her mother might love; an old photo of the town, a shawl and some blue beads. Not much perhaps, but that was no reason for her sister to say what she had, "Don't know why you bothered, she'll probably just put it in the charity bag once we're all gone. Now Mother, look at this gold necklace we've got you, it cost ever such a lot, but it's worth every penny and the children chose it specially." The children chose it specially, indeed. As if they'd chosen anything for anyone but themselves. Since they'd opened their presents, they'd done nothing but whine about what they hadn't got, and they'd barely said two words to their grandmother during the entire visit. What had happened to them? When they were small they had been such nice kids.

They reached the edge of the lake. Thin ice clasped the reeds, building glassy sculptures with little frozen tufts sticking stiffly above. The ice stretched out raggedly into the water, here just a few inches and there several feet. Pieces broke away as the wind driven waves struck, swirling in the water before disintegrating or being thrown back to lie on top of their still tethered brethren. Some geese paddled slowly, pecking at the reeds and honking mournfully. Two ducks waddled hopefully out from under one of the benches but when no bread was forthcoming they went back to huddle in their shelter.

They moved closer together and she slipped her hand into his, hoping for a little warmth. The greyness in their hearts seemed to bleed out into the landscape and the effort of talking was now beyond them. From the dark stance of woods a flock of rooks shot out and upwards. Their cawing and crying echoed off the hillside and bounced off the lake. They hurtled over the lake falling, rising, tumbling scraps of pure black playing with the wind. The sound and sight pulled at them. "Look at us," cawed the rooks. "Isn't life fun? Aren't you glad to be alive?" Just as they flew overhead one of them closed his wings and fell towards them, snapping them open only feet above them then rolling and rising, shrieking with laughter at his mastery of the air. Then they were gone.

Watery sun gleamed through the cloud. The greyness lifted just a tiny bit. His anger had faded and he shivered in the wind. "Better go back."

"Yes, we'd better. If only for mam's sake." She gave a little giggle, "Drizella and Anastasia will probably be at each other's throats by now."

He stared at her for a moment, then gave a short barking laugh, "Mind Reader."

At the house, the huge new TV was blaring loudly showing some mindless Christmas game show and her sisters clutched large glasses of wine giving loud slurred opinions about the contestants' clothes, hair and morals. The children were oblivious, staring at their game consoles, fingers flicking over the buttons, desperate to reach the next level.

Her mother was dozing in her chair in the corner, her knitting held off the floor by the few strands hitched round her wrist. At 88 it was all too much for her. God alone knows why her sisters insisted on this get together, much better if they'd each come a week apart, but then the recriminations of who got to be there on Christmas day would last until next year.

The greeting they received was as ungracious as they'd come to expect. The brother-in-law's irritated voice boomed as they came through the door, "There you are. Thought you were only going out for 10 minutes, you've almost made us late."

They were both baffled. Late. Late for what? This was the last evening of the visit, surely they'd spend it here.

"Kids are going to see that new adventure film; bought the tickets online to make sure they got in, then they can hang around the café out of our hair. We'll just sit in the hotel bar for a few hours and you can look after the old girl. I know the pub's not your thing."

Wine disappeared in quick gulps. There was a flurry of hats, coats and handshakes, "We'll just head straight off in the morning, no need to get the old girl up early. See you next year," then suddenly they were gone.

They tidied up, washed the glasses and sat quietly watching a film. Her mother woke only just long enough to go to bed.

In the morning they paid the old lady a brief visit. She seemed livelier than the day before and insisted she make them some tea before setting off on the journey home. Incongruously, a large doily had been placed over the top of the TV. She saw their glances. "It's so big. It stares at me. I thought your sister had only brought it for the boys to watch, I didn't realise they were going to leave it. I don't suppose you'd like to take it?"

They looked covetously at it for a few moments then, "No Mam. It's supposed to be a present to you. Think of the ructions there would be." They hugged and kissed her and sped off into a bright day full of sunshine and promise.

The old lady sat in her chair listening to the radio and remembering the past. She looked at the picture of the high street, the chemist's shop, now long gone, where she had her first job. She fingered the blue beads round her neck seeing the eyes of a handsome boy looking into hers, she stroked the soft wool of the shawl fragrant with the smell of tiny children long ago. Then she dozed again.

On the mantelpiece the gold necklace lay forgotten.

VISIT LONDON

Frauke Uhlenbruch

I come online in some sort of concrete alleyway.

This is different from the desert.

Gravity is unexpected, although I've done the training. A lot of training. A lot of two leg training. The commission decided in favour of what seems to be the majority mode of moving forward: two legs. My practice environment had a perfect gravity simulation and a practice body of the species. I became a pretty good walker.

But the first few steps in the real thing are different. We did the desert thing. I think most visitors do that first. Little chance of actually running into someone there. Now I'm in London and I'm *supposed* to run into someone.

***

Linda comes online in my consciousness.

"Looking good. How are you feeling?" she asks.

"Feeling. Right. Feeling! I'm fine, thank you," I reply. "Gravity is a bit unexpected. Ears did something. Found a reference, though. Apparently ears 'pop'."

Linda giggles.

"You ok on surroundings?" she asks.

"Let me just," I put one leg forward – transfer the horrendous weight of this inconvenient body – other leg forward. Once I get it started... "Let me just get out of this alley."

"You are two minutes 23 seconds two leg distance east of your destination where you are due to meet 'Kathleen' – an eligible female of the species – in 5 minutes 43 seconds," Linda transmits from mission control.

***

I am to meet an eligible female of the species. That's why I'm here. We're studying mating rituals. They mate by engaging on their binary network, called Internet. After engaging on their network, they bring their bodies to a meeting, sit through a ritualised succession of events such as food intake, and then engage in mating. The commission got in touch with this Kathleen-female through the binary network. Kathleen suggested attending a concert at a location called Southbank Centre. I think my colleagues pretended to be an eligible male of the species, named Laurence, whose body I am now inhabiting.

***

"How will I know it's Kathleen? They all look the same!" I seek Linda's advice, upon having successfully launched into walking mode and started to walk west along a grey body of water, among many other people, some of them choosing not only to put one foot in front of the other, but to speed up the process considerably, very nearly jumping forwards. A hypnotic spectacle. Linda reads my observation.

"It's called running," she briefs me. "They do it for leisure." She looks something up, then transmits an image of Kathleen, presumably taken from their network. "Run Similarity Proof. Easy. Ok, from what the linguists tell me, she considers herself to be one of the smaller-yet-wider of the species. Ethnography just informs me that that is not the ideal, so maybe don't mention it."

***

Copy that. I stop myself as I get to the meeting point. Similarity Proof alerts me to a female of the species who is sitting on a bench close enough to the meeting point and is currently using her hands to search through a small red carrying device.

I approach her.

"I say!" I say, "Miss Kathleen?"

She makes a sound that my instruments tell me is startled. Close to a vowel: o.

"Laurence?" she says and bares her teeth. Never mind. Smiles. She smiles.

"Yes, indeed!"

She makes a consonant sound this time, close to m. Then she asks, "Are you preparing for a role?"

"Shit," Linda says. "Shit. Change library! You've switched to 1930's film vocabulary!" I quickly change library.

I choose from the newly available greetings. "Yo, whazzup?"

"No no no no," Linda is losing it. "Wait! Don't say anything. Ok. Fixed. Try again."

"Sorry about that," I hear my body say. "Yes, in fact, I am preparing for a role. I'll be in 'The 39 Steps' soon."

"Oh wow! I've seen that! How cool! You know," she giggles. "This is kinda weird…"

"What is it?" I ask.

"Your name is Laurence, and you're an actor, you know…"

"I don't know what you're getting at."

Linda giggles in my consciousness. "What?!" I hiss back at her.

"This is awesome!" she transmits.

Meanwhile Kathleen looks at my body's face, then to the side, then she removes some hair from her cheek, then looks at my face again and says, quietly,

"You look exactly like Laurence Olivier in 'Rebecca'. But I'm sure you've been told that a kazillion times!"

Linda pitches in. "'Kazillion' is a metaphorical, not a mathematical number. It means 'many times'."

"You made me look like Laurence Olivier in 'Rebecca'?!" I ask Linda. It's not the first time she plays around with the laboratories' resources like that when she gets to design a body for us to inhabit. Being mainly a cultural analyst, she is mostly concerned with artistic artefacts of a given location we are visiting. Here, they have films. Linda genuinely enjoys that mode of expression. I really would have been fine with just any halfway functional body, but she simply must pick someone recognisable from their culture, as a prank.

Eligible female Kathleen blinks up at me. "Well, anyway. Shall we have a glass of wine before the concert?" she asks.

"Yes, that would be lovely. There is a charming little bar just around the corner."

Kathleen is quite pleasant to perceive through these senses. Her voice has a calming effect on this body, it appears. She looks very soft and comfortable, another thing this body doesn't mind, I'm learning.

The body experiences something unexpected. The clear building material glass can indeed be so clear that it is imperceptible through the body's visual sense. The ensuing sensation of pain upon collision causes Linda to make an excited noise, as pain was not planned to be experienced during this mission. Interesting secondary data for her.

Kathleen, on the other hand, draws in air and touches this body's arm softly, asking, "Are you okay?" in a concerned way. I reply in the affirmative.

***

Kathleen has access to a lot of libraries. I very nearly get distracted sometimes, wondering how she accesses all that knowledge with nothing but a small accumulation of nerves in her head, and maybe sometimes the aid of a device called Smartphone.

During ethnography briefings I was informed, though, that it is considered rude to use the Smartphone during a mating ritual. It is acceptable, however, to use the brain. I couldn't help but finding that notion romantic. Depriving oneself of yet one more sense when already they only have those very basic ones in order to focus entirely on the mating ritual…

***

This body experiences an involuntary reflex of laughter at a few points, and develops a sensation of extraordinary warmth towards the round soft entity named Kathleen.

Upon finishing the beverage, I attempt to get the body back into motion capacity, and am surprised about another rather unexpected development, which causes a further collision, this time with a wooden chair.

Linda explains, "The dark red beverage you just consumed is reacting with your body. Alcoholic intoxication. Nothing to worry about, will wear off before you know it."

Kathleen insists on holding on to my arm now, softly, as we walk back to the Southbank Centre. I don't mind that sturdy little second body next to mine at all, especially since the sensory perceptions of my body still appear to be influenced by the wine.

"Do you like Rachmaninov?" Kathleen asks.

"I do!" I reply. "It's incredible how humans are capable of creating such beauty for the senses and at the same time being so ruthlessly evil to one another at times."

Kathleen looks up at me and smiles warmly.

Linda comes on in my consciousness and hisses, "You're going to give yourself away with that sort of universal perspective. Remember: keep it local, national, maybe global. Don't go universal!"

"You're very wise," Kathleen says.

***

We take our seats in a hall designed to engage in listening.

I have seen footage of course, I have accessed the library of music, so there is nothing I don't know about theoretically. But it is my first time inhabiting a body which attends a live performance, transmitted not through a device, but directly into the sense of hearing.

The orchestra comes on, the lights dim, the familiar sound of tuning, a silence comes over the hall and then the first chords are transmitted directly into the body's ears and brain.

"Linda!" I practically beg for help in a desperate moment of disorientation. "What's happening? Are you getting this reading?"

"Oh," she makes, "that's normal when a male body finds a female body attractive. Your body is male. Just cross the legs and think of Baseball. Oh wait, no, in England men might think of Rugby. Those are sports. It supposedly helps with that."

But that's not it.

"No! Linda! Please, check these readings! There's water! It's coming from the brain! It's dripping out of the eyes and nose! I have to abort! This is wrong! Something's really wrong!"

She suddenly snaps alert. "Ok, calm down. Let me see."

I'm dribbling. The music being transmitted directly into my brain makes it water from eyes and nose.

Linda comes back on. "You're having an emotion!" She says, and I can hear her awe, her pure admiration. "I have never seen anything this beautiful!" she whispers.

"Help me!" I plead.

Linda catches herself. "There is a small piece of fabric called a 'handkerchief' in your pocket. Try that. It's not customary to make loud noises through the nose while using the handkerchief. Good luck!"

Just as I try to use the hand to reach my pocket, Kathleen leans towards me, with a small piece of fabric material in her hand, clearly offering me it. I take it and clean up most of the water. Kathleen smiles at me. Then her small round head is put very gently on my shoulder while her little fingers interlace with mine.

FREETOWN

Henryka Sawyer

The landing of the Boeing 767 in the tiny airport of Freetown Sierra Leone is smooth and within moments we are going down the stairs and heading the short distance on foot to go through immigration to collect our luggage. It's hot and humid despite the fact that it only just after four in the morning. The terminal is small and the officials take their time to stamp the passports, check the visas, and allow us into the country. Finally all is done and I am met by Bai Bai, the meet and greet representative working for Save the Children in Freetown Sierra Leone. He gathers not only me but also a team of three people who have come to make a documentary on the work of Save the Children. I am reunited with my daughter's friend Kat and we all head to purchase boat tickets to take us across the estuary, where my daughter is waiting for me. Bai Bai's role is done when he puts us on a minibus and makes sure that our cases get loaded on to a separate van to take us to the boat. I sit by the window and I look with interest at what is around me and chat to Kat.

The daylight is beginning to break as we descend the windy single-track road down to where we will wait for the boat. I notice that the road, or rather dirt track, is terracotta red and looks amazing between the green trees, palms and the green vegetation. I think what it must be like when the rain comes – a red river of mud. I will discover later that except for the beaches, which have golden sand, everywhere else the earth is the same – terracotta red. When we finally get to the waiting area I am surprised at what I see. There are tables and chairs, benches where you could have a picnic and there is a roof so when it rains you can have shelter and all is lit up. The short pier leading to the boat has lights on both sides of the rails and they dance in the dark water. I cannot resist and leaving the others I walk on to the small pier and look towards Freetown. The sea softly laps around me still dark in the twilight.

Freetown is covered in lights shimmering and bouncing off the dark waters giving distorted images of the city in front of me. I try to imagine whereabouts is my daughter waiting.

We wait for half an hour for the boat and when it's here we eagerly board the small vessel to take us across the estuary. The captain in his pristine uniform asks us to put the life jackets on and we start the short journey to the other side, the boat bouncing and skipping on the breaks of the ocean.

We are there and I look to see my daughter and I am waving madly and smiling from ear to ear. We hug and kiss, so pleased to see each other. She introduces me to her boss Heather and they greet the others visiting Save the Children while I stand aside and wait for Aleks. After a short time I say goodbye to the people I have met and Aleks and I head to the Save the Children jeep, loaded with my cases to make the final journey to where my daughter lives. Aleks and I keep hugging and chatting. She still looks a little pale after her recent illness. She had malaria and was very ill with it. The illness is very debilitating with high temperature and extreme headaches and it can be fatal. Treatment is easy if you know what it is that you have, as the symptoms are very much like having a bad dose of flu. Thankfully a friend of hers spent some time in Iraq and had given her as go away present a test kit for malaria. As she later quoted on Facebook – "you probably saved my life" and I thank you for that.

The roads are varied going from tarmac in places and followed immediately by terracotta red dirt track. It does not matter if the roads are wide or narrow the look is the same everywhere. There are high walls everywhere in front of which there are shanty dwellings. The roofs are mostly corrugated iron and vary in colour depending how old or new they are. There are adults and children everywhere despite the fact that it is only just after six in the morning. They are already trying to earn a living selling eggs, peanuts, fruit. I wonder if they ever have been to bed.

We arrive at Aleks's compound. For the first time I am beginning to understand what compound means. The high walls and steel gates, which I have observed on the way, guard what is behind them. The little window in the steel gate to Alek's compound opens and the guard, recognising Aleks, opens the gate and we are allowed in. The gate is shut immediately after we enter. Learning later from my daughter I discover that there is one guard on duty always during the day and that there are two of them at night time. The driver takes care of my luggage and my concentration is focused on the two pups looking down on us from the balcony. Their faces vanish in seconds and we are greeted by Tia and her sister Tess, Aleks's two dogs. They are gorgeous and I sit on the step fussing them and talking to them, they are so friendly and loving. The compound dog Monty also comes to say hello and follows us up to Aleks's flat.

I quickly look around the compound. The house in which Aleks lives is run down and in need of TLC, but not much, some repairs and paint would do the trick. It's very impressive and quickly I can imagine what it would have been like in the Colonial times. High windows fully barred, large rooms, balcony all around the perimeter, terrace on the ground floor and terraced garden all around, a private island within the walls, with electricity, running water, heating and sanitation plus ground keepers and servants. Besides the building where Aleks lives there are three others. The nurse which works for Save the Children lives in one with her partner Pete, the other is occupied by someone else who I have not been able to meet because he was on holiday and in the last lives the ground keeper with his family.

Monty, pups, Aleks and I go up to the flat. Stairs lead to the landing where Tia and Tess sleep at night. The landing leads to the kitchen and then onto the balcony. The kitchen has steel doors coming in from the staircase and also going out on to the balcony. It's a galley kitchen which has seen better days. The balcony is lovely with red floor going all the way around the building. There is dining table plus chairs by the kitchen and a settee, armchairs, and a coffee table further on. I look from the balcony at the garden below me and over the corrugated roof tops of the properties in front I see the sea in the distance.

The flat itself is very spacious. The large sitting room has wooden floor, dark oak furniture, brightly covered very big settee which can also be used as a bed, armchair, desk and there are pictures and runners hanging from the walls. The ceiling is extremely high and has a fan which is much needed in these hot and humid conditions. There also is a large bedroom with four poster bed covered in mosquito net, large bathroom with hot and cold running water, sink, storage space and separate toilet with flushing system. I imagine how it all must have looked when it was brand new.

Aleks presents me with a posy of flowers gathered and arranged by the caretaker of the compound, Pa Lamin. The flowers come from the garden and are beautiful and I am very touched.

The 48 hours with a very little sleep is catching on me and Aleks sends me of to bed. My head hits the pillow and I am asleep instantly. I wake up suddenly and it is midday but I do feel so much better. I find Aleks curled up on the balcony with Tia and Tess her two pups. We have a coffee and then do the unpacking. The cases are full of Aleks's stuff and she quickly puts it all away including my clothes and all is tidy again. After that we sit down to smoked salmon and avocado lunch with a glass of champagne – sheer luxury especially as the smoked salmon survived the 48 hours journey and all was delicious and felt very extravagant. Lunch over we decide to go down to town. Aleks wants to get a taxi but I insist on walking, thinking it can't be that far and I want to see as much as I possibly can. We take Tia with us and leave Tess behind because she is not too well and sleepy after having an injection for her ear infection.

It's all the way down the terracotta red dusty road to town and I am thinking how I will manage the journey back where it will be up all the way. It's hot, very hot. We pass at the bottom of Aleks's hill stalls selling eggs, vegetables, bread, melons and even cigarettes. The women chat eagerly between themselves while the children play around. There are street dogs everywhere lazing in the heat. They all look alike with their ears horizontal making me think of Jedai in the television advertising but they do look fed and happy. We also pass some workers building a road and they all shout to us how much they like our dog and they want it. We answer and laugh and then we have to carry Tia because she is frightened of all the noise from the diggers and the men.

Arriving in town we head first for homemade ginger beer in a restaurant Aleks knows. It is lovely to be able to have break and look down at what is going around from the balcony. Tia is happy, having had water, to sleep at our feet. There is such a buzz all around. There are children who must have just finished school in their uniforms and whiter than white shirts, blouses and socks. There people which just started coming from the mosque opposite and all in their Sunday best. It is Friday and their prayer day. The women in stunning dresses embellished with gold or silver threads and sequins all over and with their head scarves matching their outfits and intricately arranged on their heads. The colours are vivid, the dresses very fitted accentuating their figures and movements, the men in pure white gowns not as decorative as the ladies but still in their Sunday best.

Having a break was lovely and now we decide to have a look around. Aleks shows me some gallery type shops selling local woodwork, carvings, homemade jewellery. The shops are small but some of the items are incredible and we speculate about what Aleks will ship back when she leaves Sierra Leone after her two-year contract has expired. We see a little shop, maybe five feet by eight feet, where Aleks introduces me to the owner as her Mama and we look at the incredible colours and styles of the dresses on display and chat to the stylishly dressed lady. There is a small child fast asleep on the floor lying on piece of cardboard completely oblivious as to what is happening around him.

We have a table booked for this evening so we decide to head back to the flat. We walk the short distance to where the taxis are but there is a queue with lots of the school children and adults waiting to get home. The yellow and blue cars are unmistakable and they will take up to eight people to get as much as possible from a single journey. Unbelievable. At the same point as the taxis there are also bikes and with complete naivety I make a comment that things can't be that bad as there are so many bikes around. Aleks laughs and tells me that they are also taxis. I look again and to my horror I see a woman on one of the bikes holding a chicken by its wings. That would not be so bad but the poor animal is held next to the exhaust pipe and I think that it will be cooked before it gets home. I say so to my daughter, she replies that animals in Africa serve a purpose and no one thinks of them as pets the way we do and it does not matter what kind they are.

Unable to get a taxi we begin to walk back to her flat by which time I have a blister on my foot, very tired and hot. I don't give up easily so chatting we walk. Half way up the hill we see a taxi and the driver having a break so Aleks offers him more money to get us home than he would normally get in short trip. Not happy because we intrude on his chat with his friend but not been to resist the payment he agrees to takes us home. Very happy with the result Aleks and I climb into the car only to be presented with the bonnet going up and the two guys looking under it trying to start it. We look at each other and I burst into laughter, I can't believe what I am seeing but at the same time I see the humour in it. As Aleks would put it "oh sweet Salone you never cease to amaze me". My sentiment is exactly that and only after my first day here.

We are home and having a glass of champagne left over from lunch while we shower and dress. We are ready and waiting for the Save the Children's car to take us to dinner at a restaurant called Alex's right by the ocean and a nightclub called O'Casey's next to it. Aleks can book the driver any time after 6 pm to take her where she wants to go and to pick her up, as long as it is before midnight. In the taxi chatting to Lamin, I look around with interest. It's dark. The roads are now looking brown in the headlights and lot narrower then I first thought. The activity on either side of the road has not changed from the daytime. There is no electricity but all the stalls are still trying to sell their produce, their tea lights flicker and dance in the darkness. You can see the faces of the people selling their goods, still smiling and chatting in the darkness. The drive itself is challenging through all the bends, pot holes and the ditches four feet deep on both sides of the now brown looking dirt track. I have forgotten to mention the ditches maybe because I wanted to erase them, from my mind. I found them very menacing, many cars have ended in them. They are there to take all the excess water in the raining season from the main areas. They are two feet wide and four feet deep and just a narrow curb between the road and the ditch but the local traffic must know every inch between the road and the ditch.

We arrive at the restaurant and Aleks is greeted with a smile and handshake and introduces her mama. We have a lovely table by the ocean. I look around and see the lights reflecting and dancing in the dark waters of the sea not only from the restaurant but the rest of Freetown. The food is incredible. On my plate there is barracuda, lobster, giant prawns plus lovely vegetables. Aleks has seafood pie. A bottle of wine with our starter of medley of different things, and main course the bill comes to just over fifty pounds. Around the place is a display of local crafts which I find very interesting. Such variety of skills, colours, textures and objects. You can look, touch, admire and you are left to do that in your own time. Some of the owners recognise Aleks and again they greet me with their special handshake. I am touched. With dinner over and after looking at the crafts on display we head to O'Casey's bar. It's very, very busy. We go to the bar and I start talking to the owner, an Irish man loving the lifestyle he has. We order two glasses of dry white wine chatting to the owner and the wine is on the house. I protest, but don't get very far. I thank him for his hospitality. Aleks comments "I have been here so many times but never ever had a drink on the house." A typical Irishman I think. Full of life, jokes, great host a guitar player and a singer. We are having great time. I meet some of Aleks's friends, I have a picture taken with the owner on stage and then we sit and see a floor show which is magnetic. All the dancers dressed in the same fabric, almost florescent in the dim light, perform a routine which reminded me of the dancers in the Caribbean, the beat of the drums and dancing mesmerising. Total silence while we all watch the performance. Later I learn that Pete the partner of Clare is the person who finds, encourages and sometimes choreographs the routines of the local performers.

The time has come just before 12 midnight where we should take the Save the Children's jeep home, but we are having such a good time that we send the driver back and hope to get his brother to come and pick us up. He does not work for Save the Children but is now Aleks's driver and also a friend. We stayed another two hours and now when I look back it all seems surreal because it's as if we were in a capsule and as if the outside did not exist. On the way back I look at the total darkness, the road illuminated only by the headlights of the car and I reflect on the day and evening – my first day in Africa.

The next day we have late breakfast and taking the pups Tia and Tess, Lamin drives us to the local beach. The drive takes us through Freetown and I look again with interest at everything around me. The roads are busy not only with cars, trucks, bikes but also with adults, children, dogs, and there are stalls everywhere. Adults as well as children carry baskets on their heads full of different things they are trying to sell. There is a woman with a pyramid of eggs in her large basket on her head. They wander between the traffic with no urgency in their step. There is red dust and heat rising from the road and the half finished buildings serve as temporary trading posts out of the sun. There are high walls guarding smart houses inside and are surrounded by shanty dwellings. There are women washing clothes under a pipe spurting water, there are children playing in the dust, the space in which they live no bigger than a very small shed. I shake my head in disbelief and I think of the way we live, feeling suddenly very humble. We are almost at the beach and I look with incredulity at the small but nicely kept village around me. The small dwellings are brightly coloured, clean and inviting with the beach with the golden sands on their doorsteps. I can't believe the contrast from few minutes ago – unimaginable.

It is lovely to walk the Lakka beach with the two dogs darting in and out of the water and holding hands with Aleks we chat. Once again the reality left behind as if it did not exist. The locals display their crafts on the golden sand and I buy a small carved figure in ebony wood. They know Aleks and because I am her "mama" I get a free shell. I am touched but my daughter tells me that to get something free it usually means that we have paid too much to start with. We laugh and I say that I have lot to learn. The time goes quickly and we call Lamin to come and pick us up. We have a table booked for dinner and a stay overnight in a tree hut at the Chimp Sanctuary just outside Freetown.

The journey to the Chimp Sanctuary takes about an hour through the town and through winding roads leading us eventually to a point where the car can't go any further. Too dangerous for Lamin in the total darkness so the last bit we walk or rather climb the almost vertical bit of road to where the restaurant is and where we will spend the night. The incline is such that at times I think that I will never make it to the top. Aleks and Lamin laugh as I keep stopping, trying to catch my breath and saying that they are trying to kill me. The restaurant is an open room with a roof in the middle of the jungle. All around is dark except for the dim light and tea lights in the restaurant. There are ten of us to dinner cooked in a tiny space a few feet away from us. We are a little late so not having time to change we join the others and dinner is served. The meal is good but not exceptional and we all enjoy the easy flowing conversation at the table. Clare and Pete are there as well as an official from the UN, two Australian ladies and a young couple. We all have brought a bottle and at the end of the dinner Frankie the owner of the Sanctuary joins us for a glass of wine. The evening has gone beautifully and I have to pinch myself realising that I am in the middle of the jungle and about to go to bed in a tree hut. The darkness is complete and the only light comes from our torch as we walk to our designated hut. It's beautiful inside. Tiny kitchen downstairs, small shower and upstairs a bed with mosquito net, extra blankets because it can get cold at night. We go to our bag to get the camera but it is nowhere to be found. Disappointed we decide that we have left the camera at the flat. We quickly go to sleep it has been a long but lovely day. Early in the morning we are given a basket filled with boiled eggs, butter, bread rolls and bananas. We make coffee and sit on the two feet wide balcony enjoying the simple breakfast and absorbing the noises of the jungle at the beginning of the day with the sun shining and dancing in the treetops. Beautiful.

After breakfast we are taken on a tour around the Sanctuary. The guide is very knowledgeable and we learn how the chimps come to the Sanctuary. He tells us that there are places in Sierra Leone where the chimps are used for bush meat and for their skins. The mothers are killed and their babies taken and sold as pets. The problem arises when the chimps get bigger and when no longer controllable they are chained or caged getting more and more distressed and angry. The people of Sierra Leone are given incentives to report not only on the poachers but also on the locations where the young are kept. When found they are brought to the Sanctuary to be rehabilitated and released back to the jungle. It is incredible to see the animals to start with relying completely on the humans to look after them and feed them and then slowly getting more and more independent. It does take months to make them move on to the final stage of their journey to their freedom. The Sanctuary relies very much on charitable donations from all visitors as well as some funding from the government. The little craft shop attached to the sanctuary sells local crafts, carvings, hand woven blankets and throws as well as beautiful African jewellery. Looking through the jewellery I notice a huge spider perfectly poised and still between the brightly coloured beads. Thinking that it is a brooch I get a shock and jump away when it moves when I try to touch it. We buy a few items and trying to pay for our purchases Aleks discovers that she hasn't enough money. I am surprised as she is always very careful and well prepared and not having enough money is totally out of character. Lamin is waiting for us so she makes arrangements to pay the shortfall later and we make our journey back home. We look instantly for the camera and check the rest of the money at home. The camera is nowhere to be found and there is money missing from the reserve at home. Aleks makes some phone calls to the owner of the Sanctuary reporting what has happened. We don't get very far and decide to report the matter to the police so at least I will be able to claim the loss of the brand new camera from my travel insurance. We had lots of pictures on the camera so the loss was felt deeply. Aleks is distraught but I try to put her at ease saying that it is only an object and that it can be replaced. We spend the rest of the day having a nap and relaxing with Tia and Tess on the balcony and are looking forward to this evening. We are going to have dinner at the Country Lodge.

The Country Lodge is a hotel and is almost an hour drive again on good roads and more dirt tracks full of potholes. We pass stalls with tea lights still trying to sell their goods. We pass some impressive houses on the way and I am not sure if they are actually occupied. They look so ghostly in the dark. The Lodge is very impressive on the outside and luxurious inside. The large reception has gold leather settees, beautiful coffee tables, plants and crystal lighting. In the restaurant we have a table by the window decorated with heavy drapes and overlooking the swimming pool outside. There are tables and chairs and the whole area is lit up making the water of the pool crystal blue. The food is excellent and I enjoy the fresh fish on offer and the lovely company of my daughter. At the end while waiting for our driver we have a coffee sitting on the huge gold settee. We have a picture taken by one of the guests. Again I think of the almost surreal surroundings of the Lodge and think of the way the people live outside this gold haven.

It's Monday and after breakfast Lamin drives us to town to the fabric market. The day is beautiful, sunny and hot. We are dropped off and yet again I can't believe my eyes. The stalls on both sides of the narrow passage are stacked up with fabrics as far as you could reach. The African fabrics have very unusual texture. They are hard to touch, smooth and shiny having sort of glaze to them intensifying the colours. The glaze stays in the fabric even after washing. They're also very hard wearing and can be used as upholstery fabrics. We buy a lappa of this and that. Lappa is like a meter in the local language. I buy two fabrics to have two skirts made after trying one of Aleks's. Her skirt was made for the wedding of an employee at Save the Children. There is a tradition that all the ladies attending the wedding wear the same fabric made to different outfits. The skirt Aleks worn was long, very fitted and flicking from the knee down. Loved it.

We laugh and talk to the different stall owners and I have a picture taken with one of the ladies, she saying to my daughter "the two mamas". Having done our shopping we walk through the town. There is so much to see. Aleks points out to me the buildings perforated by the bullets in the uprising of 2002, the part demolished buildings – the skeletons of the war – the monuments, one of them of William Wilberforce, to the tree in the middle of the town which part of the year is completely covered by large fruit bats. The name Freetown began here where the first free slaves were brought to start their new lives. We stroll through the streets to where Lamin is waiting for us. On the way home we stop at the tailor to have my skirts made. I look with yet more amazement at what I see. The narrow street has cabins on both sides, there are animals wandering around and each cabin has the old original Singer machine inside. Most of them are operated by hand but some are really modern and have a pedal making the sewing easier. The tailors are very skilled in what they do and can copy and recreate any outfit with the most minute detail. In one of the cabins there is a chicken tied with a bit of fabric to one of the machines. We leave our fabrics and go home, the skirts will be ready tomorrow. As we leave I turn around and again try to absorb what I have just seen.

I have only three days left with my daughter and her beautiful two dogs. We go to the beach again and eat fresh lobster cooked by the local guys on the beach. The lobster and the sweet potato chips are delicious and I try not to think how the lobster was killed. In the evening we go again to Alex's restaurant but not the club and once again the food is great. This time we are entertained by a fire eating performance below in the ocean. The darkness is such that we only see the person when the torches are extinguished in his mouth. At the end most of us in the restaurant give him some money after applauding his performance.

It's Tuesday and after late breakfast of fruit we decide to do the beach in town with the pups. Lamin drives us there but we are unable to walk the beach. The heavy storm of the night before has washed all the rubbish onto the beach. I ask Aleks where has it all come from and she tells me that it gets washed down from the slums and that she has not seen it this bad before. We return home a bit disappointed but as we are going to have BBQ on the balcony we prepare some of the food and I start packing my case for the journey back. At the BBQ there is lot of laughter as well as serious talk. I still am trying to find out as much as possible as to the work both Clare and Aleks do at Save the Children. We don't go to bed until very late and the last day I finish packing and sitting on the balcony do some sewing for Aleks. I am happy not doing very much and having cuddles with Tia and Tess.

My journey back is smooth and without an incident. I sit next to a well educated Sierra Leonian and as we chat I discover that he is going to see his children in England who are in boarding school there. He and his wife lived and worked in England but decided to return back home to Freetown leaving the children at a boarding school. I listen to what he has to say and think of the children in Freetown who have to work for their living and will probably never go to school because their parents can't afford it. The contrast once again extreme and I think of the work Save the Children do by giving incentives to the parents so that they allow their children to get an education. I get to Heathrow around six in the morning and after having a coffee with my partner David we drive home.

My experience in Africa was possibly "once in a life time" but I do want to go back and to see lots more than I was able the first time. I want to see more of Sierra Leone and maybe go with Aleks into the field if I am allowed, to see the actual work that Save the Children does. I would like to see and give a great hug to the lady that "does" for Aleks, Deborah, who not only looks after her every week of the year but took great care of her while she was ill with malaria, and then Pa Lamin, coming to say hello in his Sunday best, seeing how Lamin is doing with his IT degree. I would like to go to Tribe Wanted with Aleks and spend the weekend in a beach hut and meet other friends of hers also involved in charity work. There is so much more that I would like to do. By the boat taking me back across the estuary I turn around and giving her great hug I say "I am coming back darling". I think she is a little surprised but at the same time pleased. Well I am going back in January of next year and I can't wait. There is something magnetic about Africa and I am yet to discover what it is. Maybe my next visit will give me some of the answers I seek.

CHATSWORTH QUARTET

Patricia Ashman

The man with vision

I wander by the Derwent banks
where oh so capable Mr Brown
so ordered things that every turn
revealed a vista rolling down
to these clear waters
Our eyes are taken, as he planned,
by lines he drew upon the land
Said Lancelot "Let water flow
and soothe the ear, refresh the eye
Reflections underneath the bridge
announce its progress, gliding by
this stately home
Whose many windows gaze with pride
upon this nearly countryside

CHATSWORTH: THE RIVERBANK IN SPRING

Patricia Ashman

The river here steadily grows
Released from moorland rocks it flows
through the park, its graceful course
temporarily tamed, pinned down on paper
Elegant curves running deep
under shadowed banks where whirlpools sweep
Never without sound or song
chuckling through stones, in and out,
protesting over weirs with whooshing shout
Sparkling shallows on a stony bed,
half-dry boulders stand firm
Around the base in slimy shades
the flowing locks of naiads' braids.

CHATSWORTH: THE FAR SIDE OF THE RIVER IN SUMMER

Patricia Ashman

The deer against the stark black trunks
in the shade stand still and pale
A tractor rattles, they start to move,
a creamy, billowing veil
They're running in an uphill tide
as one they flow towards the top
Curve to the right, to the shelter of the trees
drifting to a stop
High, high up at the very top,
where the land meets the summer sky

There are no trees, just the edge of the moor
where plaintive buzzards fly

CHATSWORTH: THE VIEW FROM THE CATTLE GRID

Patricia Ashman

The limited palette of January,
black, white, grey
and a surprising bright green,
the grass, shining, washed clean
by the wettest summer on record
Everywhere I look, near and far
white sheep with black ears
and ragged streaks of black tears,
like smudged mascara
on their blunt faces
Careful steps, dainty feet,
a few paces, they stop and eat
The trees are sharp paper cut-outs,
every detail crisp
against a watercolour haze,
misty, floating greys
The oaks command attention
Slowly grown, ring on ring,
gnarled heads high,
twisted twigs scratching the sky
Counting their lives in centuries,
whilst we come and go.

EVENING AT HOLME PIERREPOINT

Vikki Fitt

My bottom encased, seal-like, in its wetsuit, skidded uncontrollably to and fro on the side of the inflatable raft, and an overwhelming feeling of panic rose in my throat.

I KNEW we should have listened more closely to the group leader's talk over by the boat shed on our arrival. On a plane ready for take-off (into oblivion?) I am always the sole passenger fixedly gazing at the smiling air hostess demonstrating the emergency procedures, plucking at the safety instructions with twitching fingers, just in case... Here, I had strained to catch the critical details: what to do when trapped in an air pocket under the boat, the importance of having your stomach pumped if unfortunate enough to swallow a mouthful of the Trent and Mersey Canal, laden with toxic rats' urine. Sadly, I had failed to take in anything of life-saving importance due to the racket produced by the rabble of near-hysterical women making up our party. Theoretically, this was to be a 'fun evening' to celebrate the onset of middle-age for one of our group.

Now, after a peremptory introduction to our paddles, some bemused-looking mallards and our dread-locked guide, Lee, we had reached the point of no return, i.e. The start of the white-water rafting course. Lee, I felt, already had the measure of us; he was draped laconically over the back of the boat, speculating as to how to scare the collective pants off this garrulous, over-confident bunch. All confident, that is, apart from me, whimpering quietly near the back of the right-hand side of the dinghy. The protective helmet and life-jacket had done nothing to reassure me. I clung with white knuckles to my plastic paddle, in the absence of anything more solid to grip onto. A handle? A rope? A seatbelt?

As we circled gently in the eddies at the entrance to the course, two teenage girls leaned over the metal footbridge marking the start of the circuit and looked down on us, smirking. I couldn't help feeling that they, like Lee, were aware of the horrors that lay before us and were looking forward to seeing this noisy gaggle get their comeuppance.

I looked with trepidation at what lay beyond: churning white foam slapping and sucking at huge rocky outcrops, covered in spume, and the relentless, roaring sound of fast-moving water. Suddenly we picked up speed as we hit the first of the currents. Our squeals intensified to wild shrieks as we realised almost immediately that we had virtually no control over what was happening. I could hear Lee yelling at us over the thunder of the rapids, "Just do exactly what I tell you..."

I felt totally disorientated as we bobbed about, desperately trying to keep our precarious balance, the raft seeming as precarious as a plastic tea tray. My head and exposed fingers received repeated blows from the kayak poles suspended above us. The dinghy was swept sideways and I swiftly approached what appeared to be a deep trench in the water. I was rigid with fear and tried to stifle my screams. I heard, at what seemed like a great distance, Lee shrieking, "LEAN LEFT!" as we headed at right angles into the foaming trough.

The next second all was silent as I found myself hurled into the cascade; it was so sudden that I didn't even have time to register the icy temperature. It seemed to take an age to fight my way upwards through the filthy, greenish-brown water. The thought flashed through my mind that I couldn't drown, my life-jacket would keep me afloat, and, besides, I was a strong swimmer. My face broke the surface and I heard a brief hubbub of anxious voices. As I sucked desperately for air, my mouth filled with the fetid liquid and I choked a sit found its way into my lungs. I was underwater again. I popped up once more but had no chance to get my bearings before I was swept down powerlessly in the swirling rapids and hurled painfully against a hulking lump of concrete.

I was submerged in a giant washing machine with no way of escape. Focussing only on survival, I concentrated on breathing deeply every time I managed to struggle to the surface, having no time to think further than the next rasping intake of air.

Ricocheting from one rock formation to the next, I thought the incessant pounding of the waves would never stop. I was aware of blurred figures running along the bank alongside me, but lacked the strength to fight my way through the current to the bank.

After a seeming eternity, I heard an urgent shout behind me, a strong hand grabbed me tightly by the scruff of the neck and hauled me half-out of the water. I straddled the stern of the boat like an up-ended woodlouse, my legs flailing feebly, too weak and jelly-like to heave the rest of my exhausted body into the sanctuary of the dinghy. I tried to slow my breathing and gave myself up to Lee's reassuring hug. I was so glad to see the concerned, relieved expression on the faces of my friends.

The boat made one final decelerating spin and came to rest in the calm shallows. I had, for the first, and certainly the last time, swum the entire white-water rafting course.

ADVENTURE IN ARGENTINA

Harry Wilson

It was always in my mind to put pen to paper and write about the unusual circumstances that prompted our Argentinian adventure as well as outlining the detail of events, historical and social, that followed. All it needed was that spark of inspiration which finally emerged on the 17th April 2013, the day of the funeral of Margaret Hilda Thatcher. Part of our particularly adventurous holiday took us to the southern-most tip of Argentina, the town of Rio Gallegos, where aircraft armed with French exocet missiles flew to the Falklands and inflicted so much damage to our naval task force. Memories of the resignation of Lord Carrington, Foreign Minister, the Belgrano sinking etc., abound.

This exciting, lengthy experience was undertaken by four fearless travellers – Beatrice and Harry Wilson and Marianne and John Pritchard-Jones. In the initial planning both parties had an axe to grind, Harry wanting to visit Puerto San Julian, the location where Francis Drake wintered on his circumnavigation of the world and where he executed the treasonous Thomas Doughty... Harry is a founder member of the Francis Drake Society. John and Marianne are Welsh to the core and wanted to visit the Welsh settlements in Patagonia and, in particular, the town of Trelew where an Eisteddfod is held annually and in Welsh and Spanish. The year was 1996, the period October – November, the duration 32 days. By the way, this bold foursome had travelled the world together.

We were well aware that travel agencies would find it difficult to plan and price our complicated itinerary so we organised the whole trip ourselves. We knew we eventually were heading to an area of the Patagonian mainland, opposite the Falklands Islands so safety could be a problem. We booked ahead only 3 hotels – Buenos Aires, Rio Gallegos, near the Magellan Straight, and Calafate. Letters were exchanged with the tourist office at San Julian so they were aware of when and how long we would be staying.

Buenos Aires

Our first stop over after leaving Heathrow was Buenos Aires staying at The Continental Hotel for 3 nights. Travelling by bus from the airport to the centre of Buenos Aires we were shocked to see a massive shanty town on the outskirts of the city. On reaching the city centre, the contrast between the poor area and the gracious, elegant boulevards was widely marked. This part of the city reminded us of Paris and Madrid, as all had well-planned boulevards and public garden areas. Again, this contrasted with the narrow side streets where electric cables were exposed as were the many unsafe manhole covers.

We immediately set about walking the city centre then headed for the Parliament House, the centre of government, fronted by a large floral garden. This area featured many times on British television where mothers demonstrated seeking knowledge of the disappearance of sons and daughters by the ruling Junta. The next attraction was the La Recoleta Cemetery where the Peróns were buried, both under two metres of concrete to prevent grave robbing. Anyone who has visited the Père Lachaise Cemetery in Paris with its simple, printed layout of all buried there, would appreciate the style and grandeur of La Recoleta. Also on our 'must see' list was the classic architecture of the Colon Opera House on the central boulevard. Entry was free and the first feature to see was the wide, ornate staircase. We sat in the auditorium and visited the basement rehearsal rooms which were in use. In the evening we toured the tango dancing, street entertainers and shopping precincts dining out each evening at a typical Asado (roast) restaurant serving typical food of the region.

We left Buenos Aires, by air, heading cross country to the Welsh town of Esquel on the Andes side of Argentina stopping only once at the beautiful town of Bariloche, deep in the mountains. The weather and the town were idyllic so much so we used the name to express anything that seemed perfect. We were surprised to discover air and bus travel prices were much the same.

Esquel

The object of this visit was to see this most westerly located settlement having a population of 30,000. We stayed three nights with Rini Griffiths, a friend of a friend, who gave us the history of the area. The town lies in a shallow valley with distant views of the snow-capped Andes range. The town is laid out in American style blocks. The Indian population live on the outskirts in slum dwellings. It was of great interest to us to observe the Indian children walking to school completely dressed in white uniforms. There is no social security system so Indians must work to live. The Tehuelche Indians dominate having defeated the Chilean Mapuches centuries ago.

Esquel enjoys the services of a narrow gauge rail terminal having only two trains per week, air travel being the favoured mode of travel. We walked extensively, particularly around Lake Zeta. Trevelin is a delightful small township some 20km from Esquel featuring a well-equipped Welsh museum and an exclusively preserved original schoolroom. There is a large overpopulated cemetery all denoting names of deceased Welsh settlers.

At this stage the reader might wonder what prompted the Welsh to make such a bold decision to relocate in such a remote far-away place. At that time, mid-Victorian, many Welsh tenant farmers were persecuted by the English government. They lost their tenancies for not supporting their English landowners which materially and financially affected their standard of living. Other reasons were the domination of the English language in Welsh schools. The Argentinian government encouraged the Welsh to settle in the empty vastness of the Patagonian area of Argentina offering free parcels of land to every settler, including farm animals.

For many years, the Welsh had emigrated in search of prosperity and a better life, particularly to the United States, including a nonconformist minister, Michael D. Jones, an idealist committed to founding a Welsh colony far away from the influence of the English language and from the dominance of the Church, the Established Church. The first settlers left Liverpool in May 1865 on the 447 ton tea clipper 'Mimosa' arriving at Argentina with 165 souls on board 71 days later. Many other ships followed carrying settlers, many of whom were miners. The area of the first landing was called Port Madryn where the settlers were befriended by the indigenous Tehuelche Indians. After a few years, the Tehuelche advised that the settlers should move inland, some 60km where the town of Trelew was established. Years later, the settlers were advised to move 350km west towards the Andes Mountains where the land was more fertile and where the town of Esquel was located.

Gaiman

We left Esquel by bus en-route to Gaiman 350km to the east. This was a fascinating cross-country journey which took in many spectacular rocky landscape features. At one of the comfort stops we walked on the flat pampas observing the phenomenon of the earth's curvature clearly visible. It was at Gaiman that the settlers made a courageous decision to create two irrigation channels, *by hand*, each 125km long – 3m wide by 3m deep. These channels were fed from the River Chubut. If only JCBs were available at that time, what a difference that would have made! At regular intervals Pelton wheel type structures took the water from the channels onto the land. To me, the decision to excavate the channels compares equally to that of the Roman Wall, built by Emperor Hadrian, from Wallsend to Carlisle.

Gaiman is also noted for its numerous tea houses made internationally famous by a visit by Princess Diana. Also on our list to visit was the impressive Florentino Ameghino Dam named after the eminent Argentinian palaeontologist. Here we noted flocks of white birds, we thought were parakeets, at the town of Dolavon.

Trelew

The town of Trelew, population 90,000, is named after its founder Lewis Jones – 'Tre' meaning town and 'Lew' is from Lewis. Our visit to Trelew had been timed to coincide with the annual Eisteddfod ceremony held in a Welsh chapel and conducted in Spanish. Just to be present to observe the whole procedure, which closely followed that of any Welsh town back home, was worth the whole trip. The highlight was the chairing of the bard to the accompaniment of a highly vocal choir. Florentino Ameghino established in Trelew a museum of palaeontology featuring a dinosaur skeleton and eggs… what a find! As is our wont, we took many photographs, one in particular was the impressive monument to Christopher Columbus as well as the white stuccoed museum of settlers memorabilia, that was once a railway station.

When visiting Port Madryn there is a monument of a Teluelche Indian gazing out to sea, complete with bow and arrow, as if in welcome to the settlers. The indications are that the 'Mimosa' encountered great difficulty in landing on such a rocky cliff area.

High on our agenda was a visit to the Valdez Peninsular, some 20km from Trelew, where we planned to view whales (not to be confused with Wales!). We again travelled by mini bus then boarded a motor launch which took us out to sea to the whaling area. It was an exciting experience to witness the antics of these whales – you have to keep cameras continually poised as there is no prior warning of where whales will appear. The bulk of these nautical colossuses never quite completely leap clear of the sea and return to the deep with an almighty splash usually followed by a white spray of exhaled air. Why do they indulge in such dramatic displays? It is as if it is a playtime enjoyment submitting their bulk to spectacular antics. Are they trying to impress the opposite sex like birds showing off their plumage to attract a mate?

Also available to watch were countless seals basking on the rocky coastline. Although unseen, land animals, such as foxes and guanacos are common to this area.

Having witnessed every highlight of the Eastern settlements, we packed our bags and headed south, by bus, to Comodoro Rivadavia where we met up with a notable Welsh Argentinian whom we befriended at the Trelew Eisteddfod. We stayed just one night at this oil town (Argentina is oil self-sufficient) and proceeded by air to Puerto San Julian, the first stop on the Francis Drake section of the journey.

Puerto San Julian

As our small twin-engined plane drew close to San Julian, to the dismay of my wife and colleagues, I approached the two smartly dressed pilots requesting they take photographs with my camera of the bay, which, to my knowledge, had never been photographed before by Drake scholars, taking into account that Drake wintered here during his circumnavigation of the world. At first the pilots were nonplussed as it seemed they had never heard of Drake. My explanations fell on stony ground, particularly when I mentioned Magellan's stay at San Julian. It was my pronunciation of the word Magellan that bemused the pilots who finally and loudly exclaimed "Machellanous", the Spanish pronunciation, especially after my drawing of a map of the globe with arrows to indicate two circumnavigations. As they made their final approach to the San Julian airport each pilot took photographs completing my treasured record of such an historic setting. On returning to my seat in the plane, I was beaten over the head with magazines and handbags for scaring the pants off my friends.

At the initial planning stage of this daring adventure, I had visited the Argentinian Embassy in London to elicit whatever information was available on Puerto San Julian. The official I met had not even heard of San Julian and was taken aback when I suggested we telephone the Tourist Office there, taking into account the time difference. It was only after agreeing to pay for the call that the official put through the long distance contact. I explained to the San Julian Tourist Office the dates and times of our proposed visit and where our interests lay in relation to Francis Drake, Magellan and Darwin. Would they arrange a car to pick us up at the airport and reserve hotel accommodation for three days. All this was agreed with the lady in charge of the museum and tourism – Lic. Lucia del Valle de Lombardich, who spoke good English.

On arrival at the San Julian airport we were met by a tourist official who delivered us to the Hotel Bahia… small but reasonably clean and comfortable. We were faced with one immediate problem… there were no plugs for either the bath or wash basin. John and Beatrice were assigned the task of acquiring plugs after the concierge stated they did not supply them. They returned with plugs which were duly installed and gifted when we left thinking what a strange omission.

Lucia picked us up the following morning taking us to the tourist office where we outlined our interests. Firstly we wanted to see "The Island of True Justice", where Drake moored his ships, and where he had tried and executed Thomas Doughty. As Drake wintered there he would make use of his tents and erect huts made locally. The Indians proved to be hostile as some remembered the cruelty of Magellan, 60 years earlier.

We were taken out to 'The Island of True Justice' in a motorised rubber dinghy. A tourist guide accompanied us to the island consisting mainly of shingle. It stank to high heaven as it was now a bird sanctuary of mainly cormorants. Despite the smell we did experience some emotion either real or imagined. We returned to the tourist office and handed over gifts of hardback books on Drake, Magellan and Darwin albeit in English.

Although the majority of the terrain in the area is flat there are two prominent hills each 300m high – Monte Christo and Cerro Scholl. The two menfolk, John and Harry, decided to climb Monte Christo because of its association with Magellan who had climbed it and given its name as well as naming Puerto San Julian. The view from the summit embraced the whole of the bay including the town and 'The Island of True Justice'.

On our visiting list was the Heritage Centre which, like its counterpart at Trelew, displayed original carts and wagons used by settlers. From previous research we were aware that Drake discovered a gibbet where Magellan had hung treasonable members of his crew. A strange vignette emerged from this discovery in that a cooper (carpenter) from the Golden Hinde made a number of handled mugs from the gibbet timber presenting one to his Captain General – Francis Drake.

For the rest of our stay we were allocated a car and driver who took us on a complete tour of the bay. Again the area was largely flat and uninteresting. Our guide walked us on several beaches with not a tourist in sight. One such beach stroll was memorable... a cliff face named Cabo Curioso... this cliff face, anywhere else in the world, would be a sensation. The height would be some 30m with a third undercut by centuries of sea turbulence. The whole face was divided into definitive strata of tightly packed complete sea shells of all sizes – curious indeed. The next stop was also a bit special, it being the grave of a Lieut. Robert H. Scholl who died whilst Darwin and 'The Beagle' wintered there. The grave was rectangular and made of white palings. The inscription on the grave read – "TENENTE SCHOLL OF 'THE BEAGLE' – 20TH JUNE 1828 – AGUI YACE EL TENENTE SCHOLL OFICIAL DE LA BEAGLE, FALLICIDO LE 20TH JUNE 1828 A SU MEMORIA – LA DOTACIÓN DE LA CORBETO DE GUERA –

ARGENTINA 8TH NOV. 1890". We proceeded further and took in a closer view of the 'Island of True Justice'.

For all in our party this visit was historically significant. This area of Argentina was called Patagonia, meaning 'big feet' relating to the early Indians, named by Columbus, who were all giants.

We left San Julian en route to our next stop – Rio Gallegos which was located just south of the Atlantic entrance to the Straights of Magellan and due west of the Falkland Islands.

Rio Gallegos

Using the regular bus service, yet again, we travelled south to Rio Gallegos only being able to comment on the utter loneliness together with the shocking state of the roads, completely strewn with paper and plastic. We stayed only the one night at the Hotel Quijote. We took a stroll along the promenade meeting only a few locals until we came to a monument to the dead of the Falklands conflict. Not wishing to cause any scenes, we made sure not to overtly speak English. The next morning we ventured forth for the journey of some 250km to the town of Calafate which took us through the Parque National Los Glaciers. At one stop we viewed extensive flower displays being particularly impressed by the in-flower Chilean fire tree.

Calafate

Calafate is virtually on the Argentine/Chilean border and on the fringe of the Andes mountains. The border winds its tortuous narrow route for practically the whole length of South America. One wonders just how such a continuous winding border was created. From Calafate, situated on the largest lake in Argentina, Lago Argentinos, you have a clear but distant view of the Andes – Mount Fitzroy and Cerro Torre. We stayed two nights at the Hotel Bahia which overlooked the lake. The next day we boarded a motor launch heading for the Perito Moreno glacier, this being the whole purpose of our visit so far south.

The first glacier en route was the Uppsala much smaller than the Perito Moreno but awesome in depth and here we had to weave about to avoid ice floes. To take in all that was available to see, we dodged from side to side of the launch until we reached the Perito Moreno probably the most visited tourist attraction in the province of Santo Cruz, Patagonia. From the main viewing area, our eyes were dazzled by such spectacular, dramatic views. The glacier is constantly moving forward with repetitive, thunderous breakaways due to the effect of climate change. According to some scientific studies these glacial accumulations could disappear in 40-50 years. Seasoned climbers regularly trek on the glacier to register movements. At lake level the glacier face is 4km long.

Many people, including the writer, find climate change confusing. Its causes are said to include Carbon Dioxide (CO_2), greenhouse gases, the carbon cycle and human activity. Global warming doesn't mean in the future we will all have warmer weather, it seems that as our planet heats up climate patterns change with more extremes and unpredictable weather. Many places will be hotter, some cooler, some wetter, some drier. A classic example of global warming can be seen at Chamonix in the French Alps. In 1947 the writer has photographs of the Mer de Glace at the railway terminal, Montenvers with the glacier edge well below that level. The glacier on recent photographs has receded 3-4 hundred metres.

Throughout the whole period of this venture, we took every opportunity to talk to locals, most of whom could speak a little English, some fluent. Argentina does not have a National Health Service as we know it. For example, the Argentine government do not support the elderly, this, they say, is the responsibility of family, sons and daughters. In any case only the rich could afford the available nursing homes. Other than this the people we talked to seemed happy with their way of life.

After a two-and-a-half hour stay, we boarded the boat then back to Calafate. Returning to Rio Gallegos the next morning, we took a flight from there directly to Buenos Aires and on to London Heathrow. The whole venture is recorded by photography with the thought that one day we might return to the north of Argentina and view the Iguazu waterfalls.

Statistics: Argentina – 1996

1. Origin of name is Latin – argentum – meaning silver.
2. Population – 33 million of which half live in Buenos Aires.
3. Argentina separated from Spain in 1810 along with Peru, Chile and later Uruguay.
4. Frontiers with Uruguay, Brazil, Paraguay, Bolivia and Chile.
5. Liberator – General San Martin.
6. 90% of the population are white and principally descended from Spanish and Italian sources.
7. The pure indigenous population are Indian, representing only 0.5%.
8. Birth date of the Republic – 9th July 1816.
9. Religion – there is complete religious freedom although the official religion is Roman Catholic.
10. Currency – the peso which then was on a par with the U.S. Dollar.

CAMBODIA

Vikki Fitt

Phnom Penh to Siem Reap (Impressions from a bus)

Our public bus, purportedly air-conditioned, pulls slowly out into the Phnom Penh rush-hour (which seems to last 24 hours a day); this is the start of a seven-hour haul north-west to Siem Reap, the leafy French Colonial town which is located close to Angkor

Wat and the 200 temples which lie in various degrees of restoration and decrepitude in the jungle.

Here in Phnom Penh it's a human jungle, with something surprising, beautiful or incomprehensible appearing every few yards. Life is lived out on the streets here, and the result is a kaleidoscope of vivid colour and memorable images. Two Buddhist monks in saffron robes, bespectacled and ascetic under their golden umbrellas, greet with a Namaste a young woman swinging her plump naked baby across her hip. Squadrons of little motorbikes nip and tuck between dusty cars; some have an entire family wedged on the seat, two babies squashed tightly between Mum and Dad, riding pillion. One bike carries crowded panniers of French baguettes, a legacy of French colonisation. Tuktuks buzz along, providing a plate of pastries or fruit for their windblown commuter passengers, overtaking ponies lugging laden carts and women carrying long bamboo poles over their diminutive shoulders, filled with unrecognisable fruit and veg.

The stalls that flank every inch of the roadside purvey items from stacks of watermelons to displays of cockles, dripping with water to keep them fresh in the heat which is driving its way up to a searing 42 degrees. Stallholders lie or loll next to their produce whilst their tiny children romp in the gutter, seemingly unheeding of the traffic thundering so close to their playground. A slightly disturbing fashion emporium has a group of white mannequins with no top half, dressed in low-rise jeans with bum-crack exposed. Lengths of bamboo are being stripped alongside a woman selling vibrant rush mats, who is biting the round drum of her Buddha baby's stomach while the laughing infant arches his back in delight.

The roadside is filthy, covered in mud and plastic waste, with a constant cloud of orange dust floating across the highway; the locals wear masks to protect themselves from the pollution. The mighty Mekong River, which forms the border between Cambodia and Laos, flows turgidly alongside the road, its waters a deep opaque sludge.

As the city gradually gives way to the rural plains, the scenery alters radically. It is as dry and burnt as the Australian outback; the long-awaited monsoon will start in two weeks and the country is holding its collective breath in anticipation. The rice paddies are parched, and skinny, lop-eared white cows stand motionless in the heat, listlessly flicking their ears and tails in a futile attempt to fend off dive-bombing insects.

The colours of the landscape are a muted mix of raw umber and burnt sienna, with ochre-coloured ponds punctuating the fields, and bursts of viridian green as we pass banana trees and lotus plants, their exquisite purple and white blossoms rising from the massed greenery spreading across deep pools.

Simple houses line the sides of the road; built of wood or palm fronds, they stand on tall wooden stilts with hazardous ladders and steps, ready for the long months of rain. In the shadowy depths under the living quarters you can see the whole family carrying out their daily tasks out of the sun's harsh glare, as cows, pigs, ducks and scrawny dogs wander in and out. While the women wash themselves in big metal bowls or prepare food, their men squat beside them tinkering with their motorbikes, or, more frequently, doze comfortably in their jute hammocks. Small children are everywhere (family planning not featuring here to a large extent) and take great delight in standing at the garden well, hurling water at each other. In several plots of land there are mysterious mounds of soil close to the house, festooned with bright streamers. It transpires these are the graves of family members; their proximity must provide comfort to those left behind.

Although the paddy fields are dry, waiting to be planted up during the rainy season, there are plenty of fishing lakes. We see several farmers, wearing large conical hats, up to their chests in water fixing their nets, watched by pristine white egrets waiting for an opportunity to swoop in. Deep purple water-lilies are in full blossom. The countryside is flat but occasional volcanic hills stand out on the horizon, topped with Buddhist temples, their golden towers reflecting the bright sunlight. Tall coconut palms stand sentinel across the landscape, like rows of spiky lollipops.

The villages we pass through are full of activity; were Breughel alive today, he would produce wonderful paintings of bustling action, both in remote hamlets and in the hot, dusty towns like Kampong Thon where the bus grinds to a welcome halt to let us uncurl our crushed limbs and seek brief refreshment. The first snacks I see on the roadside market stalls are deep-fried locusts and huge black spiders. Fortunately Cambodian food is wonderfully tempting, apart from these 'niche products'.

In the space of a couple of minutes, I see the local inhabitants cooking under their rickety homes, selling, bartering, playing, gossiping, pumping water, tending crops, making, repairing, leading cattle, sitting cross-legged, tanning hides and much more, even people having a bit of dental treatment at the side of the road. It suddenly occurs to me that the scene is reminiscent of the Viking village in York's Jorvik Museum, transported to Indo-China. To me, the scene embodies an idyllic simplicity, but we are soon to discover the reality of this rural existence.

On our way to Kampong Khleang, a floating village on the Tonle Sap Lake, we have an enlightening introduction from our guide as to what lies beyond the picturesque vision we have of Cambodian life. We are fascinated to view at close quarters the living conditions of the village-dwellers in their stilted homes. The houses are extremely basic, open front and back to let a welcome breeze pass through. They have minimal possessions, but the majority have a television aerial projecting from the palm roof! Tiny children hoist themselves up the huge, steep, wooden ladders, and I wince to think of the high mortality rate that must exist here. The upside is that there is clearly a great feeling of community living. We see very few older people, we are told this is as a result of the horrendous genocide during the civil war of 1975-1979 when 1.5 million people were massacred by Pol Pot and his Khmer Rouge forces. All the professional, intellectual and literate members of Cambodian society were exterminated, leaving just a poor peasant class.

The reality of living in poverty is harsh. Medical treatment is out of the question for most Cambodians, costing hundreds of dollars to visit the (often unqualified) doctor; most doctors after qualifying emigrate to Thailand or Vietnam, where they will earn much more money. This results in the avoidable deaths of large numbers of people, chiefly children, who die from typhoid, diarrhoea and dengue fever. TB is on the increase – this is an indicator of malnutrition; when food prices doubled in 2008 many could not afford to feed themselves properly. A major cause of disease is the fact that people defecate close to the places where they are cooking and washing, and their drinking water comes from polluted sources, near areas used for toilets.

Children have a rough deal here. In terms of education, they are taught by unqualified teachers since the war (pay is low, just 45 dollars a month). By the third grade, 80% of children have stopped attending school as parents then have to pay for their education and cannot afford to do so. The result is lots of children playing around the home (we saw no toys, apart from the occasional bike), or being used as child labour – working on boats and on market stalls, or tending livestock. Childhood is short here; in the countryside girls can be married off from the age of 10.

Everywhere we see signs stating that various foreign countries have given help to set up projects to improve life for these lovely, friendly, gentle Cambodian people. However, corruption here is a way of life. Billions of dollars have been poured into the country through foreign aid, but it's clear it's generally not reaching those who most need it.

In terms of politics, Cambodia purports to be a democracy, but in reality that's not really the case. The Cambodian People's Party predominates and there is no such thing as a secret ballot, everyone knows who votes for whom. There is uncertainty about the future – the king, in his 50s, is childless (and gay?), so there is an issue about the succession to the throne. All this means a lack of stability.

Our guide is passionate about improving the situation and rightly insists that universal education is the key to the future.

THURSDAY OF THE PLANTS

Jo Manby

Walking into a small village, some forty kilometres south of the city, carrying my camera and my bag of notebooks, cassette recorder and tapes, I came across a woman and her daughter, both wrapped in dark clothes, and we fell into step. The local people had been expelled some decades previously while the country was undergoing state change. The village was located in the valley in the area where Samaria, the Plain of Manasseh and the Sharon Plain meet.

Some of the people had returned over the years. The woman told me she couldn't find her house. I asked her why not, since she must have known what it looked like; I immediately regretted my naivety. 'I don't think it's here anymore', she replied. As we walked on in silence we found only two or three original village houses remained, including a derelict late Ottoman building with its vaulting and upper-floor terrace still intact.

Over to our left was a small, temporary encampment, some women standing at the entrance to their tents, dogs sloping around. I looked back for the woman and the girl but they had walked off towards the ruined houses. I spoke to some of the women in the encampment. They had been living at one of the huge refugee camps further to the West, and had returned to their home village to find it practically uninhabitable, the meadowlands around their territory reduced to desert and the irrigation system out of use, so that nothing could grow.

Only the weeds of the steppes still flourished, such as corn bind, a relative of convolvulus that puts out its cupped flowers like little white and pink ear trumpets. It looks as if the earth is broadcasting what is going on underground – the minute excavations of grubs and insects, the blind progress of roots, the rotting of last year's vegetation – or listening, straining to hear what is going on overhead.

The refugee camp is relatively close to the refugees' original villages so many of them try to maintain close ties with relatives. It would be spring time soon. Women would traditionally have celebrated a particular day, Thursday of the Plants, around this time, whereby they would have gone out into the meadows that used to flourish around here in groups to collect herbs and flowers with which to wash their hair.

The next day they would have put on their best clothes and gone back to the fields to sit and chat and enjoy the burgeoning greenness all around them. The Bedouin women call it Khamis al-Nabat, and one woman spoke of how girls used to roll in the grass, covering themselves in dew as they gathered flowers and herbs, chanting '*Tagsh weh naqsh shu dawa el ras ya shjarah,*' which I was told was Arabic dialect for 'crack and scratch; what medicine for the head, oh plant?'.[1]

Crocuses would have been appearing, fresh and satin-bright as if thickly embroidered in silk on a cloth of woven green and ochre threads. Homer wrote about such a sight in the Iliad,

> 'With this the son of Saturn caught his wife in his embrace;
> Whereon the earth sprouted them a cushion of young grass,
> With dew-bespangled lotus, crocus, and hyacinth,
> So soft and thick that it raised them well above the ground,
> Here they laid themselves down and overhead they were covered by
> A fair cloud of gold, from which there fell glittering dew-drops.'[2]

There would have been chicory, the 'bitter herbs' mentioned in the Bible; cornflowers and milk thistles, used in traditional medicine. Although much was ruined in this place, it was still home, and the quality of sacredness about it could not simply be uprooted and taken elsewhere; it was integral to the place itself. Spirits

[1] Rema Hammami 'Between Heaven and Earth: Transformations in Religiosity and Labour among Southern Palestinian Peasant and Refugee Women, 1920-1993' PhD Dissertation, Temple University, 1994, 81-2. Cited in *Gender and Nation Building in the Middle East: The Political Economy of Health from Mandate Palestine to Refugee Camps in Jordan*, Elise G. Young, IB Tauris: London & New York, 2012.

[2] Homer 'Iliad', Book XIV verse 347, written 800 B.C.E., translated by Samuel Butler, 1898.

dwelled not only in shrines but in wells, trees and buildings, and could be called upon to aid health and well-being, to provide assistance and safety.

The woman I first encountered here at the village, who had set off for home but could not find her house, told me how she had begun the journey with her daughter, out of the refugee camp, inspired by hope. She said she had the faith that something must remain after she had lost so much. All her family except one of her daughters – who had asked, how will we know it, the house? The mother had said, it will be the only one left standing. Hoping beyond all hope.

She told me how she and her daughter had gathered together their few possessions to leave the camp; walked away, both veiled from head to toe. Their bags were stuffed with dried food, bottled water, a knife each and spare pairs of sandals. When night had fallen, cool, dark and scented, they left the camp, striking out across the sands. They walked all night, watching the progress of the stars across the arc of the firmament, aiming to camp mid-morning. Dawn had risen pink as the inside of a shell, she said, a hooded dawn, pearlised and mystical.

Far off they heard the sound of bells – a nomadic group driving their goats over the dunes. Momentarily the two parties had looked at each other across the expanse, drawn to the idea of company; then had turned and travelled their separate ways. The mother and daughter had walked and camped for days, crossing the border hidden in the back of a lorry carrying crates of hens, and had finally arrived here – found their home village and a few of their old neighbours, but no house.

Some of the women offered me a bed for the night, which I gladly accepted, not relishing the prospect of driving back to the YMCA I had been staying at. That night after settling down to the sound of quiet breathing and the movement of small animals outside, I dreamed of a long haired woman, walking into a pool of mud. Like quicksand, it dragged her down at each step. Then, as if some frames were missing from a film, I saw her face down in the mud, her hair flowing out behind her.

I was terrified but I knew there was nothing I could do to rescue her so I half turned my face away, then looked back – it was unbearable to watch. But she had flipped over and was swimming on her back in the mud, which now appeared to be more like an oil slick on water, black grease coalescing and dispersing in a clear liquid. I shouted out for help, 'Quick, I need someone strong!' but no-one came. When the woman reached the other side of the poisoned water, she walked out of the pool and onto the far bank, apparently unharmed.

I took the dream to be the product of my tired mind sorting through the events of the day – the woman unable to find her house and struggling to regain her identity; the polluted irrigation system; the contested ownership of oil in the countries of this region; but also my own role as a bystander, an outsider, a visitor. My intention had been to try to speak to some returning refugees about their experiences of finding home again. With my translator, I was able to study these women but not really to help them. Their recourse is their own strength and resilience, backed up by millennia of tradition that persist to contemporary times.

SOJOURN IN INDIANA

Harry Wilson

How many of us can recall where we were when something exceptional occurred – assassination of President Kennedy and death of Princess Diana etc? It so happened I know exactly where I was when Apollo II landed on the moon, how can I be so sure?

The year was 1969 and the company I was with was struggling to keep pace with competition as they did not have the staff with the technical knowledge to develop a particular construction equipment product. It was common practice in the industry to implement time saving short-cuts by acquisition of companies with such products.

I was commissioned to spend whatever time necessary in the United States to investigate companies who had confirmed they would be interested. One such company, located in Indianapolis, manufactured a range which, on paper, looked a likely candidate. I was met at the airport by a director of the company who advised I had not been booked at a hotel thinking I would prefer to stay in the private residence of the Chairman of the company. Little unusual, I thought, but preferable to the comparative loneliness of the usual typical hotels I normally stayed at.

At breakfast the following morning everyone was agog with excitement – timing the first moon landing – 21st July 1969. I shared with them the national pride of such a spectacular achievement. Apollo II was the first spacecraft to land humans on the moon. It was the most celebrated event in human history watched on TV by some 600 million viewers worldwide. I was privileged to be with such a large enthusiastic family on such a momentous occasion I will never forget.

The moon landing initially sparked controversy… could it all be a hoax? The American nation are, at times, easily deceived by well researched and written radio programmes dealing with just believable subjects… life after death or visitation by aliens from outer space.

Let me outline a little more about the family I stayed with at Indianapolis.

The domestic residence was in fact a large modern mansion and I was welcomed by the Chairman, his wife and a number of their children. It turned out there were 10 children living there with ages ranges from seven to 24. The first question put to me was "Do you like corn on the cob?" "Of course", I replied, so I was whisked out into the country to a farm where mine host bought a large sack of the corn to be consumed by the entire family at dinner that evening.

Having such a large family, they had to be accommodated and a complete dormitory had been built onto the house – four rooms for boys and six for the girls. The whole house was organised with a roster for cooking and cleaning, leaving the mother completely free of all the chores. In every respect the dinner party that night was something memorable. Two of the girls, the oldest and youngest, wearing mini-gingham aprons, popping in and out of the kitchen serving food and clearing up. As the honoured guest I was sat between the parents at a table large enough to cater for the entire family. At times the family chatter was deafening until father banged on the table with a serving spoon. I can't recall which came first, but we had soup and, of course, corn on the cob. This was followed by enormous tureens of beef stew, two ladles each, with comparable volumes of vegetables. At this stage I was on the receiving end of strange looks from the younger children, looks I had noticed from American children before. It was general practice to instruct youngsters to cut up food then dispense with the knife, using only the fork to eat. I was told the reason for this dates back to the cowboy and Indian periods when diners, in dire emergencies, had to have a free hand to defend themselves going for their guns. I was given this explanation in all seriousness but readers may doubt the validity!?! As I recall the dessert was Pecan Pie, a nutty dish popular in the USA. This was a meal and a family I will always remember.

For security purposes, a clicker board was placed at the main door with names of the entire family, and the last one in checked the board and then locked up.

After dinner, one of the girls advised she was feeling unwell and was concerned that her boyfriend was calling that evening on a date. This being a fun family they did not call off the date but decided to make the 14 year old sister more mature by placing two oranges in her bra, heavily using make-up and dressing her in a vivid party dress. When the unsuspecting beau knocked on the door he was greeted by the glammed up sister. "My sister is not feeling well, is in bed and has asked me to take her place – will I do?" We were all hiding behind the door to hear the reply – "You sure will", followed by peals of laughter.

Throughout the whole evening I was entertained by individual family reminiscences dominated by the love of their country, schooldays, political affiliations and, of course, baseball and football… oval ball not round!

The following morning I met up with the senior management of the company but, sadly, there was no possibility of concluding a deal.

UP AND AWAY, OR AIRPORT RAMBLINGS

Patricia Ashman

Great Hall of Worship
to the God of Travel
to unravel your cares,
walls of prayers,
read and find
your mind is overloaded
Join an orderly queue,
we all know what to do
sheep in a market pen
don't know when
slaughter will come,
they stay calm

Luggage has gone,
silently sliding on
to where? do I care?
I need coffee

Through the indignity
security scrutiny,
innocent but feeling guilty
free at last
I've passed the test slow queue to fast food

passes the time
standing in line again,
sip my drink
sit and think
check the screens and wait
Tearaway toddlers run free,
over-indulged, long over
their bedtime
Drinkers get merry
with very hysterical
laughter
Zombies linger and finger
last minute buys,
don't take to the skies
without them
Too expensive for me
to wander the shops
boredom drops from the ceiling,
slowly,
but it's free
check the screens and wait
Tedium gets worse
in this parallel universe,
check the screens
and check again
wait…… and wait
and… Go to Gate!
Oh Jubilation, Celebration,
walk with purpose
with a destination
Vast windows, light and sky,
by and by, we'll be high
up there, going somewhere,
Isn't travel exciting?…

RUTH

Peter Breheny

Ruth was woken from a deep sleep by the sound of a spade. She also heard the sound of voices, unusual because they were closer than those she'd got used to.

She wondered who it might be. At first her children and grandchildren had visited often, but as the years passed they came less often, now their visits were restricted to her birthday and the day before Christmas.

For the first few years Joseph, her husband, had visited with her eldest son but those visits gradually stopped and she wondered why. She knew he was still alive, she'd have known if he'd passed on.

When members of her family visited some stood alongside in silence, others prayed out loud, some spoke to themselves, others directly to her, reverently telling her how much they missed her.

She wanted to speak to them, but was unable to because of her condition. She enjoyed all of their visits and always listened to what they had to say as they spoke of their joys and their troubles.

In the same way she had worried about them, now they worried about their own children. They knew she understood and cared about each of them and even though they had grown-up and gone their own ways, each of them loved her in their own special way and tried to visit from time to time – but still she waited for Joseph.

Joseph was in her thoughts constantly but he never visited, perhaps it was her condition, her inability to hold a conversation or touch him made it difficult for him. Deep inside she wondered if he had found someone else, another women, she was no longer good company. If he had met someone she couldn't really blame him.

Whatever had woken her had gone now, all was peaceful again, but the air was fresher, warmer than it had been for years. She couldn't see the sun but during the day she could feel its warm rays. After eighteen years of darkness and sheer boredom she could sense a change, perhaps spring was in the air?

The very next day, Ruth heard many voices all around her, some whispered, others wept and she thought she could hear the voice of a priest praying, eventually something large was placed over her and at the same time the warmth she had come to enjoy from the sun was suddenly gone again.

A silence descended as the voices of those around her faded, but she had a feeling that someone was close and she thought she knew who it was.

From a place of silence deep within, she asked without using words, 'is that you Joseph, Joseph is that really you after all these years?' Ruth was aware of a presence but no one replied, not for a long time. Then came the sound of the voice she had most wanted to hear for so long, 'Ruth, Ruth, I'm back, will you welcome me? You know I've never loved anyone else. I was so lonely after you died. We were just company for each other.'

Ruth smiled – her time in purgatory was over, now they could cross over together.

THE GHOST OF JOSEPH WRIGHT

Nathanael Ravenlock

I've seen him. I have. I've seen the ghost of Joseph Wright. I've seen him standing calmly by the canal towpath, the late winter morning mists flowing around his body. His thick, navy, dark navy coat glistening with frosty specks, and he is handsome. As handsome as any I've seen, almost glowing when the sun breaks the horizon and the mist lifts just a touch, and I see him in all his glory. And yet, none other has seen the ghost of Joseph Wright.

"I tell you I did see him!" I enthuse as I stand beside the latest friend I've dragged out early to show them. Some smile and shake their heads in pity, some snort with thinly concealed anger and turn back home for their morning tea. But I stay there, growing colder and colder, knees and legs becoming weary and weak. I stay there hoping he will appear and then I shall know for certain. Yet my friends are already home and warm and dry as the mist clears and the ghost of Joseph Wright does not appear.

I don't do that anymore. I don't bother taking friends down to the canal to try and find him. People have lost their faith in me – if they ever had any. Perhaps they never believed me, but just humoured me. I don't mourn the loss, the lack of trust, I know now – I can treasure him all to myself, the ghost of Joseph Wright. He's mine! I look forward to those early winter mornings, for he never appears any other season, and I pray for the spring, summer, and autumn to dissolve and the air to freeze, just so it can be winter once more.

When the fog is so dense I can see nothing, I stand on the canal towpath and breathe the damp air. On it comes, his aroma, powerfully thick, melting on the tongue like sweet tobacco. The taste is rich, masculine, earthy. It ebbs and flows as the breeze tiptoes, passing through. And yet, as always, by the time the mist has danced away from the red heat of the rising sun, he's gone, just a whiff of his smell lingering – a ghostly aromatic memory.

I listen carefully as the wet from the mist strokes my face and I can hear him humming. I try to think of the tune but it is a whisper from my recollection. Still, that humming stays with me all day until the darkness of evening slowly erodes it to nothing and my heart sinks, for I might not hear his voice again for many a long day. Because, though I've seen the ghost of Joseph Wright, some winters I see him too rarely.

And then, there he is, right before me. He pauses as if contemplating *my* existence and the water laps by the side of the canal towpath. My breath becomes ragged as I ease forward, my toes balanced upon the edge, peeking over the water. I lick my suddenly parched, abrasive lips and lean tentatively out. The air tightens in my throat as my fingertips fumble to touch his form. The ice of his body crackles through my nerves, ricocheting from my bones, and I involuntarily shudder. But I do not pull away. I do not want him to think he goes unloved, so I press my palm firmly to him and my skin burns cold. With terrible, joyful tears, I weep.

I stay with my hands pressed against him for as long as I dare, and then before I leave to celebrate, I trace the words painted in gold upon his hull. My fingers tease and tickle those curves and corners, flicking where a serif leads the eye from one letter to another. The sunlight glints the outline of the name, THE GHOST OF JOSEPH WRIGHT.

He's there! I've seen him, smelt him, heard him, touched him. Look carefully and you'll see him. Down by where the willows majestically dive into the jade waters, where, if you're lucky, you catch a spark of blue as a charismatic kingfisher sparkles swiftly over the ripples. That's where you'll find him – that's where he'll find you – the ghost of Joseph Wright.

CELESTIAL LACE

Jo Manby

Pauline Eskdale feels she has spent her time wisely, working but also playing hard. She has earned enough as an actuary to keep herself in a comfortable way of life and to take time out when it suits her. She owns a large apartment in a northern city and uses one of the bedrooms as an office. She sees herself as assured, attractive, and a potentially good catch, although for the time being, at the age of 26, she is not ready for marriage or domesticity. In fact, after a decade of partying four times a weekend, she is always on the look-out for something to thrill her jaded palate.

She comes out of work one Tuesday in October, stops by the main designer shopping street and picks up an Armani skirt and jacket in gunmetal grey. She arrives home by six and tries the suit on while her laptop is connecting to the internet. She books onto a flight to New Delhi via Dubai for the first week in November when the weather there should be temperate and dry. This usually does the de-jading trick. She finds India endlessly fascinating.

Delhi airport is packed and hung with clinging scented dust, as if there is a heat haze inside the building. The winding music of a flute plays across the enchanting shudder of a tabla. Pauline waits in line thinking of the hand that might be patting the drum, or of the way a man might also pat the small of his wife's back, or, very gently, caress the upward curves of her body. Sounds that circumvent the rational mind; direct hits on the heart, the stomach, the soul.

On the first night she dines alone in the hotel restaurant. It is lavishly decorated with dark wooden panelling, sculptures based on classical Indian art shadowed in niches, on occasional tables and at either side of each set of doors. Palms and orchids throw out their opulent arabesques and a piano is being played in a different room.

After dinner, she steps outside to walk along the city streets. It is *shaddi*, the auspicious time for weddings, and grooms on white ponies with small boys riding pillion, dressed in pearls and white sequins, periodically emerge from the dusk like pale gleaming ghosts.

She enters an alley, heading north of the centre of the city. A small shop – but one which she finds to be labyrinthine inside – attracts her attention: it is selling curiosities. She is suddenly reminded of the party game where a tray of objects is brought into the room and then swiftly removed, and the children have to remember as many things as possible before it is taken away.

Only, instead of the banal everyday items such as a teacup, a comb, a pair of scissors and a toy car, here the objects are firstly unnameable to anyone but an expert, and secondly, enough to hold one's attention to such an extent that one would forget about the other objects altogether.

There is an artificial mermaid, created by curing and sticking together a fish's body, a monkey's head and an eagle's claws. Pauline puts out one finger to touch the body and an old woman appears and puts her hand on Pauline's arm. She flinches.

"Fee-jee mermaid," says the woman. "You need assistance?"

"No, thank you, I'm just looking."

The old woman shrugs and returns to her position at a small desk. Pauline's attention is drawn to a piece of gold filigree hanging towards the back of the first room of the shop. She reaches out to feel it with her fingers, and again, the old woman is at her side. The gold wire lace sends a tremor like a tiny electric shock, down her fingers, hand and forearm.

"You want? Not selling to just anybody," says the old woman.

"What is it?" The woman just looks at her silently for a few moments. "I'll take it, please." Pauline puts her hand out to fetch it down.

"Wait!" the old woman shouts. "There are things you should know. It is Celestial Lace. It is very old. It will grant your every wish and desire. But it will lose part of its pattern every time you use it. When nothing is left, Kahli comes to claim you."

"An old story?" asks Pauline.

"Old, yes. You have heard me. Now, pay, take and go. Use it wisely and no trouble coming."

Pauline takes the Celestial Lace back to the hotel, orders chai to be brought up to her and takes her treasure out of its brown packaging, laying it on the coffee table to look at it more closely. Surprisingly inexpensive, she thinks, considering that it proves to be a very finely wrought lace, sewn in gold wire finer than a hair. She can see that it depicts birds of paradise, flowers and trees. It is oval, but with points; a ten-point star. Then suddenly she remembers the wishes.

"Worth the laugh," she thinks, closes her eyes and wishes for a bottle of champagne in a cooler. With a rattle of ice and a quiet thump, there it is beside her. "Joking over then." She pours herself a tumbler-full. There's a knock at the door, and she jumps, but it is only a hotel orderly with her chai.

Trying to rationalise the situation, Pauline opens her laptop and has a good look at the British Museum website; nothing that relates to Celestial Lace. The British Library appears to have a manuscript or two with the reference. She finds the staff list and emails the keeper in question to arrange a meeting on her return to the UK.

She wishes for a handsome prince to stay with her while she's in Delhi. Then she is upset when he disappears at the end of her stay. She wishes for an extra £20K a year at work and then worries that she has been promoted to a job that she won't have quite enough experience, time or skills to do. She wishes for eternal life and gets a slap round the face from an invisible hand. She wishes to own a Titian and then is bothered to discover there's been a mysterious but major art theft from the National Gallery.

There are, however, a lot of other smaller wishes that are fulfilled apparently with no further consequence than the odd few lines of pattern going missing from the lace. Back home she decides that she needs to look at it on a more regular basis, and hauls open the second-drawer-down in her dressing table and takes out the lace. It is only half its original size. But that still leaves quite a lot to go at.

By February the initially attractive notion of serious gaming in British casinos is wearing thin and Pauline is becoming stressed about the idea of Khali and what happens to her when she reaches the end of the Celestial Lace. She keeps trying to teach herself to use it seldom and with discretion and supposes there is something like a capitalist Western gene in her that means she will carry on until there is nothing left, even though she is aware that there will be bad consequences if she does. Perhaps if she was an Indian woman she would not be so reckless, limit herself to three wishes and leave the world at her appointed hour, rather than rushing headlong towards it.

Another flight, a hotter, dustier Delhi. She returns to the shop but it has packed up and gone, another one in its place, selling house paint. It's a shock; she wanders into the Museum and asks to look at their archive. A helpful curator, Mr Jamuna, leads her past little green and yellow birds fixed inside glass cases, each one named and standing on its own little patch of twig, branch, lichen, or mineral. For what seems to be hours, he brings her manuscript after manuscript, placing them on a lectern and then stepping back courteously so that she can pore over them.

Eventually, after exhausting the possibilities listed on the yellowed 'C' index cards, themselves dating back a century, they find references to Celestial Lace under 'A' for artifice. One manuscript tells of the women who underwent the cosmetic procedure of gold lacing and the surgeons who executed it; another tells of the onslaught of frenzied hunting down of the women some years later by robbers, when the lace was taken from under their skin, without any anaesthetic, the tissue cleaned off and the gold sold, while they themselves were left terribly scarred.

Pauline suddenly realises that every mirror she has looked in has lied to her. As the gold wire has vanished, a network of scars has traced its way from around the outer curves of her face towards the centre in a spreading disfigurement. She had wondered why people had been turning away from her and averting their eyes or smiling apologetically when least required to. She looks up at Mr Jamuna with tears springing from her eyes and asks,

"Where can I get a true mirror?" The curator does not immediately reply. "I didn't know my face was so bad – I can't see it properly."

"There is no true mirror," the man says eventually. "They only estimate the truth." She sighs and leaves the museum. Outside she drops the small disc that remains of the Celestial Lace on the ground and hails a taxi. As they drive off, a small girl, dressed in emerald green and begging with her grandmother, snatches it up, her face radiant with good fortune.

THE LITTLE WHITE HORSE

Peter Breheny

The year was 1956 my brother and I were spending the summer holiday with our grandparents who lived by the sea side. Auntie Dora, our favourite auntie, lived not far away in the same town. Auntie Dora was unmarried with no children, which was probably the reason why she never forgot any of our birthdays.

At the time I was ten years of age and my brother Tom was seven. As we set off that morning, we each carried a half-crown given to us by our grandparents as holiday money. In those days half-a-crown was a fortune to a boy and worth two shillings and six pence. Just in case you're not aware, there were twenty shillings in a pound and each shilling was worth twelve pence and for two pence you could buy two ounces of dolly-mixtures and for six pence a big bar of chocolate.

Because, Aunt Dora was always kind to us, we decided to visit her and to spend some of our pocket money on a present for her. On the way we visited one of the many gift shops typical of any seaside resort.

Between us we bought Aunt Dora a bar of dark chocolate, knowing she preferred dark to plain milk chocolate. For ourselves we each bought a packet of chewing gum. At that time chewing gum was a real treat, it came from America and our parents hated it, warning us that it would rot our teeth.

Having money to burn as they say was a rare experience, so it wasn't long before we'd spent every last penny. I'd spent mine on a big penknife, which I knew would need to be hidden from my parents, if it wasn't to be confiscated.

Brother Tom had fallen in love with a little white pottery horse, which he promptly purchased for himself at a cost of one shilling and eleven pence. 'I think I'll start collecting these,' he said. 'One day this little horse will be an antique, just like the ornaments grandma and granddad have.'

Once out of the shop we hurried to one of the many benches that lined the promenade, I was soon chewing on a full pack of gum, whilst trying to extract one of the two blades from my new penknife with a thumb nail too soft for the task. The knife was so stiff, I'd soon split my thumb nail and when I did manage to open it, I quickly cut my thumb on the razor sharp blade.

As I was cutting my thumb brother Tom was carefully unwrapped the little white horse. First he unrolled the many layers of newspaper, then the soft blue tissue paper which enclosed its delicate legs. I clearly remember that one of its front legs was raised and that it had a beautiful curved neck with swirling mane.

It was a proud horse and I could see why my brother had fallen in love with it, it really was a beauty. 'I think it's one of those Arab horses,' said Tom 'the kind granddad rode when he was with Lawrence of Arabia in the desert.'

After admiring the horse for several minutes he carefully rewrapped it as the sea breeze snatched dangerously at the paper.

Like most boys we ran the rest of the way to Auntie's house. Being a faster runner, I was first on the doorstep to ring the bell set high in the big green door behind which I could soon hear the sound of her slippers on the bare lino inside the dark hallway.

Aunt Dora greeted us with big embarrassing cuddles. 'Wait, until you see what we've got for you,' shouted my brother full of excitement. 'Take your time,' she said. 'You've only just arrived, go and sit down at the big table whilst I fetch you both a drink of lemonade.'

'I bet you can't guess what we've brought for you,' Tom shouted as she disappeared down the hallway into the kitchen beyond.

When she came back, we gulped down the fizzy lemonade and because I was carrying it I handed her the bar of chocolate wrapped inside a brown paper bag. 'That's a present for you.' I said. Without taking it out of the bag she looked inside, smiled then gave me a big kiss. 'Thank you' she said. Then turning to my brother, who was still beaming with excitement, she asked, 'and what do we have here?' 'You'll never guess,' he said.

Aunt Dora carefully took the parcel from his little hands, gently she unwrapped it, layer by layer, until at last she held the little white horse in her bent and twisted fingers.

'Oh, isn't that beautiful,' she said. 'It's the most beautiful horse I've ever seen.' Then kissing him, she said, 'You really shouldn't have spent all your pocket money on me,' and off she dashed upstairs to put it safe with all her other little treasures.

When she came back down the stairs, my brother had tiny little tears in his eyes, but he never said a word and she didn't notice them.

Forty-eight-years later in her ninety-third-year my spinster Aunt died. As the executor of her will I had the duty of sorting through her effects and as you've probably guessed, in a box, in one of the bedrooms I found the little white horse still wrapped in a copy of the Wallasey News dated the 16 July 1956.

Post script: After I found the little white horse, I parcelled it up and returned it to my brother who now lives in Edinburgh.

LOVE IS IN THE AIR

Harry Wilson

What exactly is the meaning of the evocative word… love? The word has so many interpretations both physical and emotional it is difficult to be precise. The Oxford Dictionary lists some twenty-one 'words' all beginning with… love. The word itself is quoted as an intense feeling of deep emotion or a great interest and pleasure in something. Let me take you through a few examples.

I love opera, hiking, reading, skiing etc. Then there is love child – a child born to unmarried parents. Love handles, deposits of excess fat mainly at the waistline and lovelorn, unhappy because of unrequited love. I love tennis because I take great interest and pleasure in indulging in outdoor activities. In tennis and squash 'love' means a zero score. Confused as to the actual meaning? Join the club.

The origin of such an important word is said to be 'old English' and related to 'leave' or 'lief'. A bit vague don't you think! I wonder how Dr Johnson describes the origins in his first literary, history-making, dictionary. Then, what about the all too common love – love affair? The causes of this are legion – loss of interest in each other, mental or physical problems, either partner not keeping pace socially or commercially. I'm no marriage counsellor and I guess people just have to work it out themselves reverting back to the blissful courting days. You say something is – lovely – thinking it is exquisite or beautiful or wouldn't it be lovely to own a V.W. campervan? Still confused about the actual definition?

Then there is the word 'respect' which in my book means a feeling of admiration, honour or even – love. Taking marriage vows – you love, honour and, sometimes, obey!

Love sick – a pining or feeling of weakness due to being in love… and there's more!

Being born the youngest of nine, I owe much to motherly and sibling love. Whilst at school I'm sure we all had 'crushes' on teachers who perhaps unwittingly had favourites. Is this not another form of affection or love?

Yet again 'love' appears in names of flowers… love-in-a-mist… a plant whose blue flowers are surrounded by thread-like green bracts giving them a hazy appearance. Then there is Love-lies-a-bleeding… a South African plant with long drooping tassels of crimson flowers.

Again there is one of Shakespeare's lesser known plays 'Love's Labour's Lost'… love quotes are legion.

At the beginning of the First World War, my father volunteered to serve in the Durham Light Infantry. Towards the end of the war his regiment liberated the Belgian city of Louvain (Leuven in Flemish) and to commemorate the victory he named my sister – Louvain.

My sister, Louvain, and I were very close until she died, tragically, in 1939 aged only 23. Louvain recited to me the following simple piece of 'poetry' which has a permanent place in my memory:

Love is like a pork loin chop
Sometimes cold – sometimes hot.
Love is powerful, love is strong
So is pork if it's left too long.

My sister was a lovely lady but no poet laureate – there is a moral in there somewhere.

Then there is gay love which must be a bit special because such partnerships fly in the face of nature. Homosexual relationships have existed for centuries especially in Roman times. I recall reading about the popularity of bathing by Roman soldiers which was almost a religion. The Baths of Caracalla, Rome, now in ruins, located near the Coliseum and Circus Maximus (chariot race track), was built by Caracalla, son of the emperor Severus, who after murdering his brother Alba, ruled Rome with undisciplined terror for seven years. It is said that 1,000 bathed there every day. Parts of the Caracalla complex were reserved for the grooming of boys who sat on penis-shaped pegs in preparation for their masters. The other end of the spectrum was not ignored, a brothel was provided. Anyone holidaying in Rome should visit Caracalla one of the city's grandest ruins which displays classic friezes and mosaics and has regular opera performances.

Many people now support the new law allowing same sex marriages to be solemnised in Church but the Church of England clergy are seriously divided on this. Catholic and Muslim faiths oppose such liaisons. The dilemma remains.

I recall being present at Westminster Parliament when the homosexual bill was being debated. One MP stated that one in ten men have gay tendencies. Another MP rose and mischievously shouted, "With over 600 members in this house the Minister should name the sixty!"

Valentine's Day has and always will be a time for romance, love letters and above all – popping the question. The day has developed into the annual tradition on which people express their love for each other sometimes anonymously. The day, 14th February, is historically associated with love and fertility and such occasion has been hijacked by the greeting card industry.

The religious background is rarely mentioned this being the original, ceremonial thrust of St. Valentine's Day. It should be remembered a Saint is a person of exalted virtue who is canonised by the church after death. According to Catholic writing, at least three Saint Valentines are linked with the 14th February and, from my research, it is unclear why this particular day was chosen. A Saint Valentine is widely recognised as the third century Roman Saint who had a tradition of courtly love.

It is reported that in Britain alone we spend over £500 million on cards, flowers, chocolates and other gifts on this special day. Again, tradition has it that spring begins on St. Valentine's Day, the day on which birds, feathered variety, choose their mates. There are many superstitions related with romantic activities on St. Valentine's Day including… the first man an unmarried woman saw on the 14th February would be her future husband… and in Wales wooden love spoons were carved and given as gifts. Hearts, keys and keyholes are favourite decorations, such designs meant 'you unlock my heart'… origin of spooning!!

Finally, there does not appear to be any limit on bold expressions of affection. Blackpool is playing cupid with a display of shocking pink on the famous tower. Blackpool Tower is sending out a Valentine message with all over pink neon lighting to highlight the power of love… an enormous pink heart is displayed on the southern part of the tower.

The expression – 'love at first sight' has a particular resonance with me in a matter of fact sort of way. Right up to my age of 25 I had very few girlfriends; most smoked which was a major turn-off. Then I joined a tennis club in Newcastle on Tyne and when playing in a mixed doubles match I faced the opposing lady smiling across the tennis net. Then it dawned on me – this could be it! There was no feeling of lust, she was a good looker, I had an overwhelming feeling of – respect. I have to say her service and forehand stroke play was of a good standard but her backhand left a lot to be desired. I thought I might be able to help her with her problem at the same time cementing a relationship… wishful thinking. I began to think I had no hope of charming the lady but time, attention, a bit of adventure and patience finally resulted in a happy ending.

BRANNIGAN'S DARLING

Janis Clark

The night was dark
The wind was howling
Foaming sea above her bow
Brannigan thought upon his darling
Knowing he must chance it now

Boat was lowered
Despite the shining
Of the moon he sailed below
He had to land and meet his darling
And hope he would not rouse his foe

The little craft
was tossed and battered
Wildly as a raging bull
The three men knew their sea as charted
But how they wished the moon not full

On shore the cliff
Was full of action
Men and women at the brink
Saw the boat through eye-glass straining
Knew the danger should she sink

The four by four
Was quick demanded
The tow attached and brought down fast
They hurried to the bay in hiding
Saw the lowering of the mast

The sailors three
Were cursing roundly
How to make the inlet safe
The crafts outboard was coping soundly
Tho' chances were the boat would break

They tried it once
And missed their target
Once again and grazed a rock
No! No! She cried her heart athumping
In her hand his curly lock

The third time round
The sea forgave them
Tossed them in upon the bay
The helpers rushed to haul the boat in
Catching ropes along the way

Women and men
Tore upon those ropes
Hand o'er hand to fight the sea
The men on board took their chances
Leaping from their destiny

Waist high
They struggled through the water
Hand upon the heavy boat
Brannigan saw through mist and spittle
His darling's hand up to her throat

The sight of her
Gave strength to fervour
His legs moved on with greater speed
Between them all the craft was landed
The contraband they gave first heed

Once loaded up
Upon the motor
The boat attached onto its tow
The speeding car shot off with booty
Leaving the pirates down below

The sailors weary
From their exploits
Struggled up the steep incline
Unaware that forces elsewhere
Had spotted their arrival time

The coastguard
Settled in his cottage
Upon rising and prepared for bed
Took one last look through his spy glasses
And spied the small boat up ahead

His instincts showed
In this sea's rage
A boat too close than one would wish
He watched and saw the torch light message
And knew that something was amiss

He guessed the bay
And called his men out
The officers came in double time
They missed the Landy with its cargo
But found the cliff-top house assigned

The door was banged
And shouts of OPEN
Were heard above the wild wind's roar
But Brannigan's girl had forethought of them
She stripped then opened up the door

Her flimsy robe
Did first confound them
She smiled a sleepy smile and said
'Why gents, what time to come a-calling
And rouse me from my nice warm bed'

'WHERE IS YOUR MAN'
They shouted rudely
Forced her aside to let them in
'He's away from home' she said untruly
What brings you here abullying?'

Rough hands
They pushed her here and there
Brannigan raged in his hiding place
She prayed 'please God don't let him bother
They'll soon be gone, I can bear disgrace'

But Brannigan
In his lofty dwelling
The spyhole ensured he could see the trick
They abused his darling, he could not take it
Gun in hand leapt from his crib

'Leave her be'
Screamed he ascending
And shot one man who dragged her close
Another made to stop him firing
And got the same gun-fire dose

The shock stopped all
And Brannigan too
He'd no wish to kill, just save his love
But the faltering was our man's undoing
The gun was struck from hand and glove

The pair were taken
Though not for smuggling
Oh! Why not stayed your hand my love?'
Cried Brannigan's girl with copious weeping
You were safe in your secret place above

Brannigan's head
It drooped despairing
He'd been a fool and all was lost
He'd failed his love, his dearest darling
She'd been his life but at what cost

THE CHICKEN RUN

Peter Breheny

My brother and I used to climb out of the bedroom window at night after mum and dad had gone to sleep.

We would evade the local police patrols by dropping down an embankment onto a railway track, which offered a secret route from the housing estate where we lived to the surrounding countryside, where we had a den.

Close to the den was a chicken farm from where we once saw a fox wondering around one of the chicken sheds. The fox was unsuccessful in his quest to steal a chicken but it gave us an idea.

Sneaking up to the same shed in darkness we found the door locked but the window ajar. Leaning through the window I tried to grab a chicken but the chickens huddled together out of reach and the further I leaned into the shed the louder they squawked, we were afraid that the farmer and his wife would be woken up by the noise.

Just then a goods train could be heard rumbling closer so we waited until it passed alongside the farm, the click-itty-clack from it drowned all other sound, at which point I reached inside with my brother holding onto my legs. The chickens panicked and all hell let loose, the birds squawking and flapping all over the place, but I did manage to grab one.

As the train rattled away we followed along the tracks, running, the chickens head in my right hand, its sharp claws tearing at my legs, as I ran. I swung its body through the air until its struggles ceased and I knew it was dead, its neck broken.

Later we roasted it on a fire made from coal collected along the tracks and ate it in our dugout den high up on the side of "Lost Valley".

By the time mum woke us for school that chicken was history.

RAPUNZEL: THE REAL RHYME

Nathanael Ravenlock

Once 'pon a time, through the deep, darkest pines,
rode a nobleman's son, his fortune to find.
With his gallant steed of cream, white and bay,
he came 'cross a tower and there, fond delay.
It had a high window and lowly door,
and no other entrance in sight that he saw.

He pulled, he pushed 'gainst the door locked in rock,
then slipped off his gauntlet and gave dainty knock.
A face soon appeared at the window above,
the maid who'd become this sweet summer's love.
"Tis Rapunzel here, now how can I help?"
she called down to the dashing, handsome young whelp.
"I've travelled so far, I feel my journey must end,
"I seek fame and fortune, and a girl to befriend.
"Come, unlock this here door, face-to-face we will chatter."
"What about?" she asked. He said, "It don't matter."
"Then I'll let you in, but keep your hands to yourself.
"We'll talk of adventures, of friendship and of your true wealth.
"If your company's agreeable, we get on with each other,
"You'll still have to prove worthy to my protective dear mother."
The lad and Rapunzel, they talked through the day,
And when mother returned, she had much to say:
she criticised his presumption at wooing her girl,
his credentials, his lineage, his feminine curls.
"I want a real man to marry my lass
"One with manners and descendants of a much higher class.
"Now get going, little boy, before I get cross!
"And don't return here again, t'will be to your loss!"
Our hero he left, travelling all roundabout,
So he could return next day, while mother was out.
"Rapunzel, Rapunzel, let me right in!
"So I might romance you with tonic and gin."
"I wish that I could," she did awfully tease,
"But mother's locked up and taken the keys."
"Then all's lost, my love, what will we do?
"Is there no other way I can get up to you?"
Rapunzel thought hard if her prince she could aid,
Then she weaved up her locks, made a tight length of braid.
She tossed it out window with a kiss and a hope,
Praying it would make a long sturdy rope.
He climbed up the tower, hand over fist,

Then together, each other, they could not resist.
Mother found them right there in a passionate pose,
They couldn't do anything, with fear they just froze.
Rapunzel then screamed, "Don't do it, dear Mum!"
As mother kicked the lad on his exposed, spotted bum.
"Don't *dare* come back here!" Mother bellowed, in a fit,
"Or I'll flail your backside, so you'll never dare sit!"
So our hero ran off but swore to return
the very next day for his love he did yearn.
He rode to the tower through the rising sun's glow,
Then called up to his sweetheart in that skylight window.
"Rapunzel, Rapunzel, let down your hair,
"You know I can't get to you by using the stair."
"You crazy, my man?" she did so reply,
"I've just had a wash, a cut and blow dry!
"My hair is all gone, it's been taken and sold,
"To make my mother a mountain of gold."
From up in her tower she spied his bay horse,
"Is there room for two on that pony of yours?"
"Of course," he replied, "My dearest, my dear!"
"Then be patient, my prince, for I've got an idea."
Into her knickers she tucked her long skirt,
So when she fell down she'd not get terribly hurt,
She jumped from the window with a cry and a hoot,
And her skirt ballooned up like a great parachute.
As she floated down she had a bright thought,
I believe I've just invented a brand new, scream sport.
She looked at her prince, shouted, "You might find this funny.
"But I know of a way we can make a stack load of money!
"You buy this tower, Prince, straight off me mum,
"And we'll show them rich tourists hours of fun!"
Adrenaline junkies came from far distance lands,
They paid silver and gold fist over hands,
To have a go at this wonderful thing,
The real dangerous hobby of base-jumping.

THE PEOPLE'S THEATRE

Harry Wilson

It was when I was 20 and in the fourth year of my five year indentured apprenticeship that I was transferred from a machine shop lathe to the marking-off tables in Seven Shop at the Scotswood Works of Vickers and Armstrong's Ltd. This move was part of the apprenticeship scheme of things and still a job in overalls. As I had not performed particularly well at Rutherford College I thought I would never be called upon to make the final move – into the white-collar drawing office.

Much to my surprise the call came and I was interviewed by the Chief Draughtsman of the Scotswood Jig and Tool office. I was rejected due to my poor exam results and the fact that I was left handed – a problem in those days as all draughting machines were for right handers. My next interview was at Elswick Works – with a Mr. Bert Waggott, Chief Draughtsman of the engineering office working on naval gun emplacements aboard warships – I was accepted.

At school I had taken part in a number of plays and I noted on one of my annual school reports (which I still have) that my teacher had commented "has dramatic ability". The only part I can remember having played was that of Ebeneezer Scrooge in Charles Dickens' "A Christmas Carol". This gave me the taste for acting and I long held an interest in joining a theatre group and especially the People's Theatre, Ryehill, Newcastle. One night I plucked up courage and made my way to Ryehill to find out what it was all about.

The theatre was a converted church with the auditorium where the pews had been located and the floor underneath where the Sunday school and choir practices were held. This lower room was converted into a rehearsal room, wardrobe area and a Green Room – a noisy meeting place.

So, at 19, this was the scene at Ryehill that greeted me on that cold, damp Friday evening at about 7.00 pm. Facing the front entrance of the "church" were two entrances with two flights of about eight stone steps up to a formidable, large double door which led directly into the auditorium. To the right of the flight of stairs up was a similar flight down and at the bottom was a smaller double door which led into a 10-yard or so window-less corridor with box office windows on the left and on top right, two swing doors… the entrance which was to become a character-building wonderland of the theatre.

That fateful Friday evening I descended the flight of stairs, gingerly opened the lower door, entered the dark hallway and I could hear music and more than a murmur of many raised voices. I hesitated at the swing doors for what seemed ages but could be no more than a minute, and considered a panic retreat. But Geordie pride prevailed and I eased one swing door slowly open and stepped forward. The noise of such animated conversation was deafening, a cacophony of male and female voices which scared the hell out of me, and I tried to retreat but was halted in my tracks by a young woman who invited me in. That young woman was no other than Elizabeth Trower (nee Kelly), wife of Peter Trower, a leading light in The People's. Betty Trower was responsible for welcoming new members and as far as I was concerned she certainly did that. I was duly enrolled as a member and initially visited the Green Room about once a week. At the all too tender age of late 19, brought up in the Blaydon "streets", intermediate and not Grammar School educated, living in a Council house and a factory worker in overalls, embarking on an absorbing artistic recreation made me think I was a little out of my depth.

The furnishings in the Green Room had not been purchased at Harrods and had to be seen to be believed. Tatty old rugs were strewn across the floor. The fireplace was the focal point of the large room with two three-seater sofas placed at right angles to the fire and six to seven feet apart. These two sofas, whilst being continually occupied, were anything but comfortable. The springs pierced well into the moquette although not actually protruding. I doubt if the sofas had been cleaned from new. All this gracious furniture reflected a homely atmosphere and that the People's had very little spare cash, hence the importance of getting the maximum number of bums on theatre seats.

A large portion of the Green Room was, in fact, the Wardrobe Department and controlled by the strict, no-nonsense but loveable wardrobe mistress, the chain-smoking Alice Hands. Well stocked with period costumes and if a particular dress or jacket was not in stock Alice would get it. Alice was respected by all and a round peg in a round hole.

To the side of the fire was a large door which led into a spacious, much utilised rehearsal room. At the rear of this room was a door which led into the back street and children living in the area were often a nuisance, disturbing the concentration of the actors.

So much for the building, activities and furnishings – now for the people who made up the People's. All types gravitate to an active theatre group, myself being but one. I met so many members in the first weeks I had great difficulty in fitting names to faces, especially the few who were from overseas. I recall one evening sitting on the much loved sofa, carefully avoiding the protrusions, and reading, when a body quietly came alongside. Looking up I saw a middle-aged, distinguished looking gent. Being in such close proximity I thought I had better introduce myself – "My name is Harry, Harry Wilson" – shaking his hand. "Glad to meet you Harry – my name is Wolf, Wolf Mankowicz." I was immediately upstaged – me with a surname third in popularity in the 'phone book behind Smith and Jones! How I envied his Christian name, comparing the power of Wolf to happy Harry. I considered a change of first name to Wolf or Wolfgang, but decided against it, being a skinny 5ft 7ins and admitting to myself I could not carry it off. We had nothing artistic in common, but subsequent conversations centred on Tottenham Hotspur and Newcastle United. Wolf worked for the B.B.C.

I made many friends as you do in the compact world of the theatre and to name but a few – Mary Pigg, Wendy Kennedy (afterwards Watson), Ella Brace, Jack Kavanagh, Nick Whitfield,

Bill Scott, Norman Darling, Frank Kirkham, Bill Nicholson, Len Scott, Dorothy Burdis and Harry Tuff.

Bill Scott, a rounded, competent actor, became a good friend. So much so we went off to Stratford booking accommodation through "The Stage" which was alongside the theatre entrance. We saw three plays and were very impressed with the quality of acting and staging, particularly that of Romeo and Juliet. Bill wrote a booklet he named "It will be quite alright on the night" and very funny it is too. Last performances of plays give rise to levity and I was on the receiving end of Bill's sense of humour many times.

A charming couple took my eye – John and Doreen Pleydell. I saw John march into the Green Room in a Lieutenant's naval uniform. My first thought was that he was in costume for a full dress rehearsal. Next "sighting" he was in mufti as he did not want to get his uniform soiled – he really was a "proper" naval officer. John started his naval career as a midshipman and after a few years training at Portsmouth, Greenwich and at sea, he was confirmed Lieutenant towards the end of 1942. During his time at both Scotswood and Elswick Works at Vickers-Armstrong's he had became a Gunnery Officer, about January 1944. It was at this time they joined the People's having long been interested in the theatre. Doreen had worked for H.M. Customs and Excise and they married in April 1942. We were in a number of plays together and I particularly recall the Whitsuntide gathering at Wallington Hall, the home of Sir Charles Trevelyan where we entertained the Trevelyan family, and they us.

Another "foreign" name to conjure with was Heini Przibram, pronounced "Sheebram"and his Geordie wife Rommi. I have to admit that I was in awe of this formidable couple. Rommi was tall, elegant and a beauty whose wide eyes looked straight through you. A graceful lady, this being demonstrated many times on stage. Heini was also tall, was dark and handsome with it. His slight accent was one of his attractions and I recall thinking he would make one potent villain if any such role came up. I hasten to add that much later in our lives I learnt that his looks belied the true character of the man.

Heini was born in Vienna on the 6th January 1918, which, making a not too difficult calculation, makes him five years older than me. Heini arrived in the U.K. in March 1938 and married Rommi in August 1943. Heini achieved his B.Sc. in Engineering in 1941 and in 1942, when I joined the theatre, he worked on the Team Valley Trading Estate, Gateshead with Sigmund Pumps, a company I knew well.

Rommi came from good Geordie stock, not that Heini was in any way inferior. Rommi's father was the founder and Chief Executive of a successful advertising agency. Rommi read Chemistry and Physics at University and met Heini there. Both had a great sense of humour, which surfaced during the production of Xmas party sketches. When you're 20 and in the theatre, five years age difference is 25% older and therefore positively ancient. As actors I could see they were a class well above mine.

Another impressive theatrical gentleman was Henry Davy and even more "ancient" – at least 15 years older. Managing Director of a large printing company, he was also an author, writing the play "Boy from Vienna" with his friend and later mine, Peter Trower.

I have already mentioned the first person I met on entering the portals of the People's was the charming Betty Trower – Mrs Peter Trower. I was fortunate that Peter and Betty took me under their wings both theatrically and socially. Peter was to produce a play at a small Gateshead theatre and I was offered a minor role (my first ever) in "The Dover Road" by A. A. Milne, also author of Winnie the Pooh. From there I was offered a few parts in People's productions and I suspect the Trowers' had a hand in this.

Coming into Ryehill straight from Blaydon "streets" I must have been a wee bit raw with a Geordie accent. No author springs to mind who wrote classical drama for Geordies so something had to turn me into a budding John Gielgud. Betty suggested a few sessions with a prominent People's leading lady and highly qualified elocutionist – Marie Hopps. After five to six free half hour sessions, she must have re-arranged my vocal chords to produce sounds from Blaydon to High West Jesmond. In order to illustrate how to control sound and volume output Marie explained the function of the diaphragm, took my hand and placed it firmly on her flimsy silk-clad tummy, almost flesh to flesh, commenting "feel where my breathing is controlled". I have to say that being a mere 20 year old I got quite excited for the wrong reasons. Marie got rid of the raw part of my Geordie accent. I still have a copy of Marie's book "The Spoken Word".

I was an invited guest on many occasions for weekends at the Trower home at Moorfield Road, Jesmond. On one such visit, at breakfast, Betty suggested I help out by attending to the toast, pointing me to the new kitchen cooker. First, I had never seen a modern cooker and had no idea where to put the bread slices. At home, at Blaydon, I used a toasting fork against an open fire. I put the bread in every visible aperture, without success – Betty had to show me how.

I was invited to accompany the Trower family on a number of picnics and one such outing I remember well because the location was near a wood at Riding Mill on the upper reaches of the River Tyne. Whilst it was a very happy day, part of it was infuriating. Why? Betty and Peter introduced me to the 'game' where they gestured "the moon has a round face, a nose and a mouth" describing a circle round the head and pointing to the nose and mouth. Every time I did *exactly* as they did they shook their heads… wrong! I did it so many times – wrong – I was spitting blood. If anyone reading this would like to know the secret, let me know or send an e-mail. How I enjoyed and appreciated the friendship of the Trowers!

After leaving Tyneside, a married man in 1952, I lost touch with Betty and 35-40 years later (Peter had died in 1967) I finally tracked her down to Elstree where she was playing Auntie Nellie in the T.V. soap "Eastenders". I have so many happy memories of my time at the People's I could turn this simple narrative into a lengthy novel, particularly the Whitsuntide visits to Wallington Hall and the many highs and lows of the plays and players.

Half way through the year 1942 I joined the People's Theatre at the age of 19. Long after I married and left Tyneside I could not remember much about the plays I was in or the years in which they were performed. All was revealed when Wendy Watson, a People's stalwart, sent me a copy of the book "The Peoples" by Colin Veitch.

In this last season, I was 26 and was obliged to concentrate on my career but I continued to visit the theatre but only as a member of the audience. I finally lost track of the theatre in 1951/52 when my wife and I moved to Manchester.

Prompter's Notes

For the duration of any play, prompters, in their lonely corner of the wings, usually have an uneventful time. They have their own exclusive copy of the play and would have studied the script, particularly the leading parts, stage directions, pregnant pauses which produce dramatic effects. They must have an unobstructed view of the entire stage. Prompters come into their own when an actor 'drys' and be watchful for entrances and exits. Usually the prompter's role is avoided like the plague and awarded to anyone who volunteers. Ideally the prompter should attend some rehearsals but always the dress rehearsals.

Every prompter has tales to tell and coming from one who was press ganged into the role a few times, here are one or two from my own or others' experiences.

1. The play was 'The Tempest' and I was playing the part of Ferdinand, opposite Miranda. In a woodland scene I carried on my shoulder a real heavy log and met up with Miranda. Final performances are a bit special and the cast sometimes take liberties. On the last performance someone substituted a realistic balsa wood log for the real thing and on stooping to take the strain of lifting the heavy log, I lifted it and it shot over my shoulder much to the amusement of the audience and the prompter.

2. The only time I can recall 'drying' was in 'The Wild Duck'. It was the second performance and well into the first act when I panicked – I could not remember my next line. If you move on stage the audience is not aware of any problem. I walked over to the drinks cabinet, poured a drink, turned and said "How are things in the timber business?" which was all I could think of. The other actor on stage looked daggers at me, went to the drink cabinet, poured a drink, turned and said "Fine", thinking, no doubt, you got into this mess you get out of it. After what seemed 10 minutes, but actually was perhaps one, the prompter finally caught up. For years I thought it was my fault until a recent reunion when an old friend, Jack Kavanagh, mentioned how sorry he was for me as the 'dry' problem was not my fault as another actor had missed an entrance – delayed action relief!
3. Audiences be warned! Avoid second night performances. For the first performance actors are keyed up and are usually faultless. For the second performance, over-confidence sometimes prevails resulting in a lack of concentration, which is manifested in 'drys'. I hasten to add that this applies largely to amateur performances, professionals would not allow this to happen.
4. Some actors, when they 'dry', snap their fingers until the prompt arrives whilst others actually walk off stage, get a prompt and walk back hoping the audience has not noticed anything unusual.
5. During the Priestley Play 'When we are Married' which I produced in a Benwell Church Hall, a stage 'flat', which housed a fireplace and mantelpiece collapsed on stage when an actor leaned against it. The prompter was non-plussed when the actor said "Remind me to get that fireplace fixed!".

My active period at the People's Theatre lasted 7 years and I enjoyed the whole experience – acting and helping with stage management, making many close friendships. Every member at one time or other assisted in making renovations and painting stage 'flats'. I will never forget the smells both of the stage area and the Green Room – glue-size, paint and the special smell of damp hessian… smoke, tea and coffee and that faint odour of old carpets and settees. There can be no doubt that the whole People's involvement helped to shape my character, boosted confidence and greatly improved my vocabulary.

After leaving Vickers-Armstrong and the sedentary drawing board, I applied for jobs that normally I would have thought beyond my capability and, trying not to be too 'dramatic', this self confidence lasted right through my career even to taking the decision to invest in a manufacturing company with two friends, eventually selling out in 1995.

As a consequence of my final and full retirement in 1994, and my success in tracking down Liz (Betty) Kelly, Beatrice, my wife, and I met Liz at Elstree and later at her home at Scarborough. We endlessly reminisced about our time at the People's Ryehill in the mid-forties to mid-fifties… it was such a pleasure recalling plays and events during that special period. It was as a result of the meetings with Liz we were made aware of the close proximity to Ashbourne of the Pleydells at Knutsford and the Przibrams at Wrexham. This sparked off the idea to organise reunions at Newcastle of old members active in the forties/fifties era. Three reunions were eventually arranged attended by 60/70 old members. They were all happy occasions which featured choruses of "How are you?" and much genuine embracing. Henry Davy and Wendy Watson organised the Newcastle end with dates coinciding with theatre productions.

It was a particular pleasure for me to meet with old friends like Jack Kavanagh, Nick Whitfield, Mary Pigg, Ella Brace (Kingston that was) and regrettably so many well known faces were missing. At the new location of the theatre, a Jesmond cinema, the Green Room and bar are a great improvement on Ryehill as was the vast area, by comparison, of the reception and meeting place where we congregated for the reunions. Had I not finally met Liz Kelly I would not have been put in touch with Przibrams and Pleydells. In addition to the reunions we have met numerous times – 3 couples – and hope to meet again in May 2003.

In this narrative I have hinted that my complete theatrical experience gave me the background enabling me to write countless sketches and a number of stage and radio plays. I must admit I am more at home writing about historical subjects. My full length stage play 'Axe Must Fall' was about the incarceration of Mary Queen of Scots and her eventual demise at Fotheringhay Castle. The play was produced at Stafford Playhouse in 1988.

Being a founder member of the Drake Exploration Society, I have researched all of Francis Drake's achievements. I am hopeful that my radio play 'Drake's Justice' will, eventually, be recorded.

Elizabeth (Liz) Kelly, her real and stage name, was a successful actress, now aged 92 (2013), she lives at Scarborough. Throughout her stage career she played many lead roles but she will be most remembered for playing the mother in Laurie Lee's 'Cider with Rosie' at the Contact Theatre, Manchester in 1982.

The Theatre Critic in the Manchester Evening News said after the first performance: 'But the evening, above all, belongs to the marvellous Liz Kelly as mother. Choose your own superlatives. I cannot praise her performance highly enough, she's the right actress in the right play at the right time giving what is probably the performance of her life'. Later, the play toured all over the country.

Liz spent happy months in the BBC Radio Drama Company and among her TV work she is most remembered as Aunt Nellie in East Enders.

GEOFF'S MUM

Peter Breheny

This is a true story. Some time ago a friend of mine went to visit his aged mother who had been rushed into hospital. At first he was very concerned about her, thinking she might be on her last legs, but as the days passed she improved and as she improved his jovial sense of humour returned.

Geoff the Chef, as he was known to his many friends, was a large, happy and generous man who when visiting, as well as taking gifts for his mother also took gifts for all the other old ladies who shared the ward with his mother.

Geoff didn't just take one bunch of grapes. Geoff took bags and bags of grapes. So one day when his mother asked for a box of her favourite sweets he came with enough for everyone in the ward.

Sweets were handed out to everyone and for once the ward was full of smiling faces until Sister Killjoy came into the ward. 'What idiot is responsible for this?' she asked pulling no punches. Geoff stepped forward, 'thought I'd cheer them up a bit, sister.'

'Cheer them up, are you mad? Most of these patents are diabetics, do you want to kill them?' At this Sister Killjoy raced around the ward collecting all the sweets, mumbling and grumbling as she went.

From that point on Geoff made the most of winding the sister up whenever the opportunity arose. You could say a love-hate relationship developed between them, Geoff had been put in his place but he wasn't one to let someone like Sister Killjoy get the better of him.

When the day came for Geoff to take his mum home he arrived at the ward dressed in motorcycle leathers carrying two helmets. 'Are you ready mum? I've brought the bike and sidecar; it's a lovely morning, thought we'd drive home through the lanes'.

Geoff proceeded to wrap his mother up in several extra pullovers and a big leather coat several sizes too big for her. He turned-up the collar and wound a big woolly scarf around her neck until all that could be seen were her eyes peering out over the top of the collar.

'Well that's about it mother,' he said, helping her into a wheelchair, we'll just go say good-bye to the sister then we'll be on our way.' The sister took one look at her patient trussed-up in the old leather coat with a crash helmet on her lap and exploded.

'Are you completely mad Mr Bartlett? Your mother is eighty years old, a small and frail woman still getting over a serious illness and you plan to take her home from hospital on a motorcycle.'

Her face became bright red as her anger surged – 'Over my dead body.' Then as the rest of the family entered the ward, all with big grins, Sister Killjoy realised she'd been set-up.

MOZART REQUIEM

Vikki Fitt

Quite when it was that Cupid's arrow struck me I find difficult to pinpoint now. I remember it as being about the time that I was emerging from bovine motherhood. Years of undiluted Calpol and fascinating discussions about mastitis over gritty instant coffee had left me in a state of domestic insularity, where excitement consisted of a major success in the long haul to potty-training, or the elder offspring successfully auditioning for a part as a choral vegetable in the primary school musical production.

Then, gradually, the thick mists of full-time motherhood started to evaporate and I became aware there was Another Life beyond the confines of my four-bed des res with Aga, a life that, before hormones took over my mind and body, had involved the world beyond, a world that included culture, film, theatre, literature; a world that I was set to rediscover before the major part of my brain atrophied.

One of my first forays into the world outside was to the cinema, where the film of 'Amadeus' was causing controversy with its radical portrayal of the life of Mozart. I was transfixed by the whole production, the music (naturally), the setting, the romance and wild dissipation of the characters. In the weeks that followed, I became a Mozart junkie, surreptitiously squandering large amounts of my housekeeping money on Naxos CDs. I could rise above the squalor of the nappy bucket while listening to the Requiem, or turn up the divine tones of the Piano Concerto No. 21 on the (admittedly crackly) car radio and drown out the sound of squabbling siblings on the back seat.

I needed to extend this new-found joy in music to my children. OK, so I'd missed the chance to lull them to sleep in their cots to the sound of The Master, but it wasn't too late to develop their cultural sensitivities and get going with some music lessons. The choice of instrument wasn't exactly democratic; Georgina would have preferred a blast on a trumpet, but for the sake of our collective family sanity I insisted it be my old viola, festering in its tatty old case since I stormed out of Junior Orchestra more years ago than I cared to remember. I duly obtained the number of the viola teacher recommended by school, and arranged for lessons to take place on a weekly basis.

Well, on the big day I was the only one to show a vestige of excitement and enthusiasm as we waited for Mr. Clark to arrive. Georgina would have been far happier to rot on the sofa till bedtime, stuffing her face with Monster Munch after an exhausting day struggling with Roger Redhat and Jennifer Yellowhat, and the trauma of her papier-mâché balloon self-destructing during technology. As I heard the throaty roar of his car engine (a nice soft-top Golf GTI or NVQ or whatever the model), I dashed to the back door to let him in.

What a dish! Late twenties, open-necked shirt but nice suit with appropriate aura of professionalism, carrying a black leather music-case. But, best of all, a dead ringer for the young Wolfgang Amadeus, right down to the tumbling, sun-kissed ringlets. (Actually, I'm not sure Mozart had sun-kissed ringlets because normally you see him with one of those wig affairs on but you get the idea. And, anyway, the film had taken liberties with his appearance…). I stood listening in the kitchen to the excruciating sounds Georgina produced on her first attempt; our 18th century walls weren't thick enough to mute the full horror of an uncontrolled stringed instrument but I suppose even Yehudi Menhuin produced caterwauling like this at an early stage. I resolved to relocate 'The Music Room' to a more distant corner of the house for future lessons. In fact, the term Music Room was a trifle grandiose for what was an old honky-tonk piano from a junk shop, a triangle, a plastic gazoo and a collection of assorted percussion instruments mainly constructed from combinations of Fairy Liquid bottles and lentils.

Mr. Clark paused in the kitchen, ostensibly to chat pleasantly to me but more basically to receive his fee (well-deserved to my mind, considering how close he'd had to stand to the source of the noise). I went straight into my role as domestic earth goddess, looking fetching and pink-cheeked in my blue gingham pinny, a nutritious boeuf Bourguinonne simmering temptingly on the Aga behind me. As I entranced him with tales of my own musical career (Grade 2 piano, recorder club at school etc.), I flung my stripy oven gloves over my shoulder with gay abandon and leant back against the sensuous warmth of the stove, determined to keep eye contact with him for as long as possible. He smiled patiently as I chuntered on with details of domestic trivia, and I thought to myself how much I would treasure his weekly visits and these intimate moments in the centre of my cosy domain. Suddenly, I noticed his gaze slip from mine, his eyes opening wide as he stared in horror over my right shoulder. Reluctantly, I stopped ogling him with shameless adoration, turned and realised my oven gloves had caught fire on the hotplate. The ensuing activity was chaotic to say the least, with copious amounts of water being hurled around the kitchen and my playful banter replaced by something a lot more earthy. Mr. Clark retreated from the conflagration as quickly as was decent.

The risk of being burned to death didn't deter him from returning for future sessions, and gradually the tortuous sounds from 'The Music Room' (now in the spare bedroom) became slightly more tuneful. However the day came when we had to accept the fact that the Royal College of Music was not going to be fighting to offer Georgina a scholarship for services to stringed instruments, and anyway, she was more interested in mini-rugby (which suited her father's aspirations much better). Sadly, I had to concede that my Thursday afternoons would no longer hold the same appeal, and that the day-dreaming and happy anticipation that kept me going through the week would disappear. Regretfully, I paid Mr. Clark off.

Several months later, I had recovered my sanity and was back at the educational coal-face, my period of full-time domestic servitude now at an end. One frosty late-autumn morning on my way to school, I dashed into the Esso garage for a quick petrol stop, rushing in the manner that had become a way of life since taking up the challenge of running a home and a career in tandem. A familiar voice spoke from behind me; there was the young Mozart, tossing his ringlets, filling up his soft-top at the adjacent pump. My heart stopped momentarily and I heard my voice take on that tone of girlish laughter it always adopted when I was talking to him. He too looked highly amused, in fact as if he were about to burst out laughing, a state of affairs that I optimistically put down to his sheer pleasure at seeing me again. We chatted amiably, for as long as time would allow, then I realised just how late I was and padded over to the service station shop whilst Mr. Clark roared off in the opposite direction.

I shivered slightly. It was colder than I'd thought this morning. Then, standing in the queue for the till and seeing my reflection in the polished window, I realised to my horror just why: in my rush to leave the house earlier, I'd made a last-minute dash to the loo and had managed to secure the back of my skirt firmly inside the waistband of my tights. Instead of smiling with pleasure at the serendipity of our meeting, Mr. Clark had been trying to contain his laughter at the sight of my nether regions encased in Marks and Spencer tummy-trimming Lycra. I would never be able to look him in the eye again.

I've moved on to Beethoven now.

SILENCE

Peter Breheny

I drive along a dirt track
Seeking peace and solitude
At the end of the track
A gate leads into a field

I reverse up to it
Facing back, in front fields
Drop gently into a valley
No road is visible

No motor hums
Momentarily I close my eyes
Open my ears
Aware only of buzzing flies

In and out of the open window
Tickling my nose and eyes
No songbird breaks the silence
Waves of grass move gently

A butterfly flutters
There is no sound
This place is silent
Comfortable, without stress

No dream visits my sleep
I could be dead
Unaware of life
Nothing exists

Until, in the distance
A crow caws
A bird chirps
A sheep bleats

And suddenly across the sky
A jet bound for Manchester roars
Its passengers gazing down
Looking into my secret world.

WARTIME ENCOUNTERS

Harry Wilson

In 1943 the tide of war was turning in favour of the Allies. Towards the end of January 1942, General Montgomery triumphed at El Alamein and in January 1943 the Germans surrendered at Stalingrad. Despite repeated bombings of Tyneside shipyards, arms factories and random targets, life seemed reasonably normal. Theatres and dance halls were thriving and the Newcastle United Football Club continued playing every Saturday afternoon with guest players, some members of the armed services. Food and clothing rationing had been accepted and was working equitably and who would have believed we would find so many ways of cooking the American humble delicacy – SPAM. The People's Theatre, Newcastle, like the Windmill Theatre in London, kept open throughout the war. The theatre programme carried the message "In the event of an air raid the play will continue but should you wish to leave you will be escorted to the nearest shelter."

I was 20 years old and in the fourth year of my indentured apprenticeship working at a major arms company, Vickers Armstrongs Ltd, Newcastle. At that time my main activities were the theatre (People's Theatre) and ballroom dancing, having been coached in the latter by my older siblings. At a lecture on 'The Art of Acting' at the Newcastle YMCC in mid-1943, I met Gordon Lea, the lecturer. Gordon Lea was then a well-known playwright for work on stage and radio. At the end of the lecture, Mr Lea invited questions and, to my later amazement, I stood up and asked "What do you think about the Stanislavski method of acting?" After the lecture, Mr Lea approached me to ask if I was active in the theatre. I replied, "Yes – The People's Theatre, Ryehill, Newcastle." He then enquired if I would agree to accompany him on his lecture tours taking part in play reading. He was very interested in my association with the People's stating that one of his full length plays had been produced at Ryehill. After some thought and not without apprehension, I agreed to accompany him little knowing what I was letting myself in for.

It was on Saturday 9th December 1944 when Gordon Lea, who was also accompanied by a young Lieutenant, in uniform, also named Harry, was giving a lecture to the Rothbury Women's Institute on 'The Theatre' that a disaster took place. Midway through the lecture, without warning, Gordon collapsed vomiting volumes of thick blood over the stage ... he had suffered a burst ulcer. There was uproar with many ladies fainting or leaving the hall in great distress. Lieut. Harry, in uniform, the other companion of Gordon in our party phoned for an ambulance and we escorted Gordon, pale and silent, to the Rothbury Cottage Hospital where he stayed for a few days.

On returning to Newcastle, Lieut. Harry driving Gordon's car, the young officer told of an amazing undercover operation in Northern France which ended tragically. Lieut. Harry, I was not made aware of his surname, was kicking his heels waiting for his unit's next assignment when a notice was issued asking for volunteers for a dangerous mission. The timing of this notice would be sometime in July 1944 shortly after D-Day. Eight men volunteered including Harry and a sergeant. After rigorous fitness and explosive training, including parachuting, they familiarised the drop area and boarded a small American aircraft for a night operation.

The brash American pilot involved ribbed the Brits practically the whole of the short night flight shouting at the jump time "Good luck – you'll need it." Unfortunately the pilot was way out in his calculations of the recommended drop zone and Harry and his men just could not recognise the drop area, finally establishing they were some 50 miles from the target area. They were to blow up strategic targets to harass the retreating German army, this with the help of the Free French Force.

Not having anticipated this new situation, Lieut. Harry decided to split his unit into two groups, he in charge of three men and his Sergeant the other three. They were to converge on the target area in a pincer movement travelling at night. They set off in their different directions not knowing when and if they would reach the target zone.

Lieut. Harry had ordered his men not to forage for food during daylight hours but, after a few days, he learnt later that the Sergeant could not control his men and all four were captured and summarily executed as spies. Lieut. Harry had a similar experience with his men who foraged during the day, were caught and also executed, he being the only survivor. He headed to Paris to make contact with the Free French Force, succeeded but was interrogated and tortured as they believed him to be a German agent. He was finally accepted and the allied advance was such that in August 1944 he was standing on the Champs Elysees watching the liberating army's triumphant march to the ecstatic cheers of the Parisians.

Lieut. Harry reported the conduct and gross error of the pilot in regard to the drop zone to his superiors who, in turn, made representations to their American counterparts as this miscalculation was directly responsible for the loss of seven volunteer soldiers. I never met Lieut. Harry again after Rothbury and I did not check the validity of his account of his undercover mission largely because his military unit or his surname was never divulged. At no time during our long traumatic day at Rothbury did he mention anything about his mission other than to say he was on extended leave. It was when we were driving back to

Newcastle that I asked questions about the war and why he was on extended leave. He then gave me a detailed account of his failed mission after which I asked if he would be in line for a medal to which he replied 'You don't get medals for failure."

Is this remarkable story true? On balance I think it was. Lieut. Harry was in uniform, on long leave, and it was only after persistent questioning that he poured out the story and as a friend of Gordon Lea I don't think a liar would have lasted long.

It took Gordon, by now we were on first name terms, some four weeks to recover from his ordeal when he turned his attention firmly on to me. He rarely engaged in face to face conversation with me as I could not afford a car, lived with my mother and sister, Charlotte, in a council house without a telephone. I was now 21, still an engineering apprentice at Vickers-Armstrongs, Scotswood, still in overalls whilst Gordon was in his early 50s, clearly well-educated and a man of substance. So the fascinating letters started. Long letters, letters in rhyme, letters in the form of a play between him and me. He invariably and gently insisted I should write back to him but I was bewildered and way out of my depth. How could I reply in kind with me barely educated and he a published author and the leading authority on writing radio plays.

Just what on earth did he see in me to write such friendly, intimate letters. He was unmarried, living with his mother and I read into that that he was probably homosexual, now known as 'gay', who, for some reason, had taken a shine to me. I never encouraged it nor did I ever express such affection as he did. I had no gay leanings, indeed the complete reverse. I really began to feel sorry for Gordon as I just could not respond in like terms.

Gordon wrote six long letters, together with a few shorts, all of which were special. Most of the time we talked on the phone... a kiosk at the corner of my street... when I was mildly harangued for being so 'neglectful'. In the end I had no choice but to stay silent and the letters from Gordon petered out. I still retain all his beautifully crafted letters, in his own handwriting, and saddened that it should all end this way. Years later I decided to trace

Gordon's home address... Horndean, Low Fell, Gateshead and located a large Victorian house set in a spacious garden front and back. Looking at the impressive mansion I thought of what might have been had I been so inclined.

MOHAMMED BOUAZIZI

Janis Clark

Mohammed Bouazizi, what have you done?
Your actions have caused the prime minister to run
Did you know then what you had risked
By raising that metaphorical fist?

Your army rose up, that's what you did
By showing the people and not keeping the lid
On your anger and frustration at being poor
And by shocking the world, who saw. They saw.

Your people were with you in spirit and mind
When they heard of your gesture and your sad decline
They knew that somebody had to pay
They saw who you were and you led the way

But, Mohammed, do you know
How thousands have died since your firey show?
You set in motion an endless string
Of massacre and murder – THE ARAB SPRING

Your God will decide if you were right or wrong
Only *He* can judge where you now belong
But those who suffered and were not free
Shall honour Mohammed Bouazizi

LEAVING THE SUN BEHIND

Frauke Uhlenbruch

Driving through the foothills that separate the valley from the coast, you'll notice a strange weather phenomenon. Just before you get to the coastal road you're on a plateau. The sun strikes down from a cloudless sky; the grassy prairie landscape looks yellow and scorched. Soon you will come through a small town – not much more than a post office with its paint chipping off. Driving along a highway through burnt meadows under a blue sky, here, in this small town, you will notice a bank of clouds hovering where you know the coast is. There is no horizon, just a wall of white. Land meets clouds. The road takes you right into the clouds and from one second to the next it becomes so foggy that you have to switch on the car's headlights.

The coastal road winds along on top of a cliff of indeterminable height. Seagulls may be keeping up with you. The sunshiny road trip music becomes redundant. You suddenly feel the need to accommodate a silence.

Maybe you've started to fly, unaware.

A few miles on you can leave the car in an empty gravel lot. A footpath leads down the cliff to a sandy beach. It's windy, chilly and foggy. Waves roar. There are sharp rocks off the beach.

Nobody's here.

This beach is neither for surfing nor for swimming nor for tanning. It belongs to the seagulls and the seals, which will occasionally lift their curious faces out of the water to spy on this intruder.

When you take off your shoes, the sand will feel warm under your feet. As if only minutes ago the sun had still beat down on it: a ghostly remnant of former warmth. Now it's hard to imagine how you ever managed to get sunburnt. It's amazing how quickly a body forgets that it was ever hot, how quickly it will forget that it was almost shivering on that rugged beach facing the raging waves: all forgotten when you drive back out of the dreamed cloud landscape into the heat under blue skies on the plateau you've left behind.

The air is filled with salty mist and the din of waves crashing against the ragged rocks. Seagulls perform aerial acrobatics.

Nobody's here.

I stand in the surf until my feet hurt from the icy cold water.

Nobody's here. I take myself out of the equation. I'm just a guest.

GRANNY NICHOLLS

Peter Breheny

In 1950 when I was four years of age, we had a neighbour called Granny Nicholls who was eighty-six years old. By my calculation that means she was born in 1864 at the same time as the American Civil War. At that time Granny Nicholls was the oldest person I knew by far older than my own grandparents.

As children, when we were ill, Granny Nicholls would appear at the door carrying a jam jar covered with grease-proof paper. The jar would be full of a substance she called gruel, which was her answer to all ills. It looked like porridge mixed-up with beef gravy and my mother would encourage us to take it although from what I remember it was usually thrown away not long after she had left.

Granny Nicholls would jokingly tell our mother we were spoilt and needed to be disciplined, with the cane, but for all of that, we loved the old lady and liked to visit her in her flat where every Tuesday she would clean what she called her treasures. Mum said that Granny Nicholls had worked in service as a young woman and explained that in the old days working class girls like Granny Nicholls would leave home to become servants in big posh houses owned by toffs.

My dad said that they were nothing less than skivvies to the idle rich and it was clear to me even then, that this was a class of people my dad hated. Another neighbour called Mrs Price who lived next door always referred to my dad as 'The Master' a term he found highly offensive, pointing out to me that it was people like them, the Price's, that wouldn't join a trade union to fight for the rights of working people. Later, I found out that my grandmother on my father's side had also been in service to a doctor at Blundell Sands near Southport before she met and married my grandfather, a proud and independent Irishman.

Granny Nicholls was a Catholic like us and when the Bishop of Shrewsbury was over on his three year visit to confirm the children of the parish, Father Murphy our parish priest brought him to visit her. We all knew from Granny Nicholls that he was expected, so we hung about in the street, with all our protestant friends to see him. It was an amazing sight, the bishop left his car and driver down at the end of the street to walk through this predominantly Protestant estate displaying the flowing robes of Rome. In close attendance was Father Murphy who pointed out the homes of the few Catholics, identified by the image of the Sacred Heart displayed behind the small window in each front door.

We all hung about outside Granny Nicholls flat, he was there for about half an hour, when he came out Father Murphy pointed out the Catholic children to him, but he didn't speak to us, just gave each of us a fleeting blessing as he passed. One of my Protestant friends asked if the bishop had been turning him into a Catholic, saying his dad wouldn't be very pleased if he had.

Within minutes we'd rushed in to Granny Nicholls flat to find out what the bishop had said to her. She was laughing and told us when he arrived and saw she was about to kneel to kiss his ring he'd told her not to, but feeling it was the correct thing to do, had gone down on one knee. The only problem was, she couldn't get up again, so the bishop and Father Murphy had to heave her up which she found hilarious.

One Tuesday we went round to see her treasures. Granny Nicholls' flat was really interesting to us, because it was full of interesting old pictures and ornaments. She had lots of silver cutlery and every Tuesday she polished it. First rubbing on a white liquid, which set all chalky, we would each be given a duster to polish it all away, being careful not to leave finger marks on it. When we asked why she always did it on a Tuesday, she said that was the day she had to do it when she was in service and that she'd carried on doing it on the same day ever since.

Amongst the silver we cleaned was a silver medal with a bar, we knew about bars because my dad had one on one of his medals, it meant he'd won it twice. Granny Nicholls told us the same story every week, the medal had been won by her first husband who had been in both the Boer War and the First World War. The Boer war she said had been in South Africa where he'd been fighting the Boers who were Dutch settlers that lived in the Orange Free State. She used to tell us how the British soldiers all had bad stomachs because they never had time to cook their food properly before the Boers were chasing them again.

When I asked my dad about the Boers he said they were very cruel people who were very bad to the black people and explained that the medal was a very special one called the Military Medal, which he'd won twice for bravery in the First World War and which was almost as good as the Victoria Cross.

After the medal was cleaned came the best bit, she would open a cupboard and take out a long bayonet for cleaning, this was the best bit of the job. Did your husband kill anyone with this, we would ask, is there any blood on it?

One Tuesday she was telling us all about the cavalry and how when they went into battle they had set exercises that they would go through using their swords so that the enemy couldn't sneak up from behind and stab them in the back. She stood in the middle of the room, the bayonet in her right hand, swinging it left to right, right to left over her left shoulder behind her right and down across the front. Then in her excitement she plunged it down into her leg above the knee. Blood seeped through her fingers as she pressed down in a vain attempt to staunch the bleeding, we looked at her. I'll be alright she said but within seconds, against her wishes I was running down the stairs to fetch my mum.

At first my mum blamed us thinking we'd done it, but Granny Nicholls said it was her own fault. The doctor was called out and after he'd seen to the wound and Granny Nicholls had explained how she'd been going through the cavalry exercises, we all had a good laugh with the doctor.

Granny Nicholls took ill a few years later and died suddenly, at the time she was the only person I'd ever known who had died. After the funeral her son, a nice man who always wore a suit gave my mum four solid oak chairs, which were still in the family fifty years later.

TRAILER PARK

Jo Manby

It will be the year a Pan Am jumbo jet crashes onto the town of Lockerbie; the year gay rights protesters invade the 6 o'clock BBC news; the year pubs will be allowed to open all day in England and Wales. Two of your friends are going to ring you tomorrow when they get back from hitchhiking across Africa, south to north. They will be coming home across the Mediterranean. Another will have just returned from paying a visit to the Dalai Lama. You and your friend Helen are only going to be asked back to someone's place for coffee after meeting up in a nightclub. Red leatherette banquettes; girls dancing round their handbags, still in their fast-food outlet uniforms; white stucco; green and pink neon. Or you might be going to meet them outside a pizza takeaway, Pablo's or Pepe's, where you'll be cadging a late supper at 3am, teasing the lads standing around on the pavement: 'Surely you can't eat all that yourself?'

You will need to get out of town anyway. There's going to be a fight going on around you, two stag nights clashing limbs and foreheads on the cobbles;

'Hey, that's my ex – what're you doing with him?'

'I think you've got the wrong bird, mate, she doesn't know you'. You're not going to be a part of it but it's going to start encroaching on your space. The space around you that you feel is your own personal Venn diagram, with you at the prominently-coloured central intersection, your friend Helen and your sometime boyfriend Michael occupying the two other circles, the third circle your life. The fight will be on the periphery but it'll be violent and arbitrary.

'Come on, let's go', Darren'll say. 'Car's just outside the wall.' You'll drive into the river of lights; orange, red, white; green for go. Names will flash by: Esso, Shell, Spar, Mace, Massala Queen, Tandoori Nights. Eventually the river will go back to source, just a few cars now, thinning out, one or two drivers will be speeding like you, one or two over-cautious after drinking. To start with you'll head for a semi in the suburbs. You and Helen will sit on the backseat of the Fiesta. The suburbs'll run out and Darren and Nick will tell you it's going to be a ground floor housing association place.

You won't be unduly worried although the thought will strike both of you that this is not a very sensible thing to be doing. There will be some discussion going on in the front seats but mostly it'll be a subdued drive. There won't be any sign of the housing association place. Outside the outer estates they'll tell you it's a flat. You'll be expecting a high-rise. When you finally arrive it will be a static caravan in a trailer park.

'Do you live here, then?' Helen'll say. 'Blimey.' Dogs will bark at the other end of the park. The soft pounding of music will carry on the wind that will rush in the trees and a cow will low for its calf in a neighbouring field. Darren will ask Nick if he has his keys on him and then make a lame joke about the possibility of them both having locked themselves out. Darren will flick a light on and gesture to the seats – more banquettes. 'Fancy a drink?' he'll ask. They'll have one bottle of red wine but no glasses so you'll have to drink it out of teacups. Helen will start to get bored immediately. You both will, only you're better at covering it up and being polite. You won't be able to help admiring her unabashed honesty.

'You can cut that out for starters', she'll say. She'll be pushing Nick's hand off her knee. 'I don't go for your type.'

'How about him then?' Nick'll say.

'No thanks. Got any fags?'

'You've smoked the last ones.'

'Got any central heating? We're froz sitting here, aren't we, Caz? Got any champagne or smoked salmon? Know how to treat a girl, don't you?' Nick will blush and Darren will kick at the carpet with the toe of his pointed boot. Darren will work himself up into a self-righteous rage.

'What's up with me?' he'll ask. 'What's so wrong with me then? I'm young, I've got a car, I've got a decent job, I've got my own place, I'm good looking. Why don't you fancy me?'

Helen will begin to laugh. You'll try to explain that it's not as simple as ticking boxes, it isn't a question of multiple choice, you have to hit it off with someone, there has to be chemistry. 'Why can't you hit it off with me, then? I'm young, I'm good looking, I've got a car and a job and my own place, what's up with me?' Helen's eyeliner will start trickling down her cheeks as she snorts with laughter. You'll feel sorry for the lads but there'll be no redeeming the situation. You and Helen will look at each other. Time to go. 'If you're expecting a lift back to York, you can forget it,' Darren'll say. Helen'll come back with 'Don't worry, we aren't.'

You'll step down from the caravan onto the concrete paving and into the warm spring night, sober but amused. The road will be quiet when you set off for home. You'll only see two vehicles, one will be a lorry and you'll both just ignore it, hoping the driver isn't going to offer you a lift, and the other will be a police car. It'll stop and the driver, Sergeant Something-or-other, will ask you what you're doing walking along the A1079 at 5.30 in the morning. You'll explain that you're on your way home and ask him for a lift, but he'll say, 'Sorry girls' and tell you to mind how you go, which you'll both agree is a bit of a cheek.

When the dawn comes up and the birds start to sing, you will already be near the outskirts of the city. Under laburnum trees dripping yellow gold along a factory wall you'll come across a cat that will have been killed by a passing car and Helen will insist on giving it her version of the Last Rites before you go on your way. You won't see Darren and Nick again.

MUSINGS ON OLD AGE

Vikki Fitt

I recently went to the cinema to see a new film release, 'Quartet', a heart-warming and visually beautiful story of a group of elderly retired musicians living together, generally harmoniously and definitely well-cared for, in a gracious English country house. Their efforts to put on a fund-raising gala result, of course, in a triumph, with any personal difficulties neatly resolved: the requisite happy ending hoped for by the 'cauliflower-heads' (as my daughters would fondly describe the predominantly superannuated audience).

As we shuffled out of the auditorium there was a common theme running through people's sotto voce mumblings, my own group of middle-aged friends included.

"Why can't it be like that in real life?" we muttered wistfully. "Let's all live together when we're older, pool our resources and live together, yet independently, with company and friendship on tap." I think we all had a similar mental image, that of an existence like that of a student living in a hall of residence, but with better food, cleaner bedding, a much better quality of red wine (RIP Bull's Blood) and a ready-made social whirl (even if the activities on offer would be more sedate and Zimmer-friendly than in those hedonistic days of yore).

Two things really resonate with me from seeing the film. The first is the emotional force that was produced, not by the sentiment or the satisfactory resolution of the story, but by the impact of the closing credits. All the actors, not just the A-list stars, had their name and photograph on the screen; next to each was a vibrant portrait of these elderly performers in their prime, octogenarians and beyond who, decades previously, had been leaders of world-famous orchestras, prima ballerinas, operatic divas swathed in bouquets at Covent Garden. Each was recognised as not just an 'old person' living in care, but an exceptional individual who had excelled in their own artistic field.

My second observation stems from a short piece of dialogue from the film. The once-famous soprano whispers sadly, "I used to be someone once," to which her friend replies "I thought I still WAS someone!" This resounded strongly with me, and it keeps coming back into my mind, not least when visiting my 92 year-old mother in her nursing home this week. Of course I know my own Mum's back story, her hinterland, a whole tapestry of life. Not world-famous in any respect, but a unique individual who demonstrated a range of wonderful personal qualities and skills until physical and mental decline finally overtook her. But as I sat with her in what is effectively 'God's Waiting Room', I chatted as always to the other residents, trapped in their wing chairs. Audrey, bright as a button but afflicted with Parkinson's Disease; Peter, wandering around in his pyjamas and licking his plate, dignity gone; Harriet, suffering with a bad hearts and problems 'down under' which she delighted in sharing with us in excruciating detail over lunch, but determined nonetheless to make it to her 100th birthday in four weeks; and finally Maddy, always smiling and thrilled to see you, whose main joy in life is feeding the voracious pigeons outside the window. All these are individual characters too, each with their own history. Their stories deserve to be heard and their uniqueness celebrated, just like those talented performers in 'Quartet'.

THE SONG OF THE MILL

Patricia Ashman

The mill has been silent for many years
Though the stream passes by his door
She is singing still
But she and the mill
Aren't on speaking terms anymore

Long ago they chattered and laughed
And made lively music together
Water splashing and bright
They would sing with delight
In wet and stormy weather

When the stream met the mill, the wheel came alive
And then began to turn
The building shook
In each cranny and nook
As the water began to churn

***

Cogs on the pit wheel
meshing with the wallower
turning the main shaft
and great spur wheel
Spur wheel and stone nut
working together
turning round the runner stone
on the top floor
Higher up the main shaft
crown wheel turns
sets off the belt drive
hoisting up the sacks

Once on the top floor
grain falls by gravity
into the hopper
on the first floor
Pours into the middle
of the moving runner stone
ground on the bedstone
into flour
Spilling from the edges
falls into the tun
then all the way down to the ground
where it had begun

***

Proud of these memories, the mill stands tall
Hoping that someone will unlock the door
Then the day will come
When the timbers will hum
As he and the stream sing their song once more

FADING FLOWER

Nathanael Ravenlock

She sat there in her battered chair, in her small flat. She was thin; thinner than he'd ever seen before. Her hair was equally thin, and combed straight, where for years it had been dutifully curled. Her age had always been amusing considering her good health, but now reality crept in. He had never known her so quiet.

"We're going to have to leave now, Gran," the young man said, kneeling down next to the old woman. He took her hand in his and could feel the bones through the skin – skin blotchy and veins narrow and raised. "We've got a long journey ahead and…" he glanced back at his wife, standing by the door clutching their swaddled baby, "the little one needs his bed."

"Thank you for bringing him," the old woman finally said.

"Of course," the young man said, "we will bring him again soon." The old woman turned her head to look at him. "We will bring him again soon," he repeated.

She shook her head slightly. "I won't be 'round," the old lady whispered, "The Lord is coming to take me." And when the young man said nothing, the old woman looked into her grandson's eyes, searching. "You used to believe." she said, "When you were a child."

But I grew up, he thought.

He said, "I will never forget what I was taught."

The grandmother gave a weak smile and looked away again. "He will take away my pain, like your little one has done today."

"Then we'll come again soon," the young man said. He looked at his wife and she forced a smile. He pulled his hand away from the old lady and stood.

"No," she said firmly, not turning to look at him, "there won't be an again. The Lord will take me tonight."

"Don't be like that, Gran," the young man soothed, "you're recovering well for your age."

"My age. My age. My age," the old woman tasted the word, "my *age* is what *ails* me, my boy." She turned to look up at him, "Why can you not see it's my time? This world is no longer mine. I leave it gladly to your little one. I wish to be with the Lord." She stared hard at her grandson, "He will come, you be sure of that."

The young man felt uncomfortable under her gaze.

"We need to get the little one home," he said softly and then bent down to kiss his grandmother on the cheek. "We love you, Gran."

She smiled. "Help me, my boy. Give me another pill before you go."

The young man picked up the small container from the table beside the old woman and read the label. "It says three a day. Haven't you already had two?"

"Yes, but I can't open the lid myself," she said, "and the doctor's not calling til tomorrow morning."

The young man nodded and pushed down on the cap while twisting it to release the child-proof lid. He tipped the container, tapping it against his palm until several pills rolled out. He pushed them all back in, except one, which he placed on a plate on the table.

"Just this one," he said, putting the container back on the table and then placing the cap beside it, "You understand? Gran? Just one. No more."

She nodded, smiled and reached out squeezed his hand.

"Goodbye, Gran." The young man whispered as he stepped away.

He walked to stand by his wife and they left with their child. Before he closed the door he glanced over to the old lady, who was staring at the wall once more.

When the door clicked shut, the old lady looked down at the open pill container, gave a satisfied grin and closed her eyes.

MEMORIES

Henryka Sawyer

The little house built entirely of wood stood on the edge of a large orchard and looked deserted and engulfed in darkness. The flickering light which you could just make out came from the small oil lamp placed on a tiny table in the middle of the room, the house. The oil lamp was the only source of light, there was no electricity, no running water, no bathroom; it was just a single room with two small windows and a door. The room was all there was to that house, it contained everything – two single beds, the little table with two chairs, and a stove which served also as a bed in the cold winter months. The stove was built out of bricks and tiled on the outside, the top had some rings on which the cooking was done and once the embers were dying out it served as a place on which you could put a small child and keep it warm through the night. The darkness outside was complete, no stars, no silvery shadows of the moon which was on that occasion totally obscured by the evenings clouds.

The silence shrouding the place was unimaginable, unreal. Inside in the dimly lit room it was no better although two young people were there. The young boy of about fifteen was busy boiling a jug of water for a drink for him and his little sister, silent and huddled in the very far corner of the bed. She sat there with her knees tightly held by her small arms, silent, staring at the door as if waiting for the door to open and for someone to walk in. The young man was very good looking, handsome, almost six feet tall even at his young age, with striking cornflower blue eyes, full mouth, dark hair, perfect features and physique. The little girl was about six years old but looked much younger simply because she was very petite in all respects. Her hair also dark, cropped below the ears, her eyes almost black like two pools in the tiny face.

They were both silent, preoccupied with their own thoughts because today was the day that they buried their mother and now there were only the two of them.

The mother died of tuberculosis, a disease so very common forty-five years ago. Her absence from the little house was not uncommon as she spent most of her time going in and out of hospital. The children were used to fending for themselves, the neighbours helping many a time with a jug of milk, flour, potatoes or a piece of meat on some rare occasions. The little girl was quite happy eating fruit from the orchard, sleeping in the hayloft when her brother was not about. But today was different – their mother will never enter that house again, never cook "pizzy" the child's favourite, nor give her a cuddle or see to her scrapes and scratches or talk to her son ever again. Yes, today was different, today they buried their mother and both the children seem to be actually waiting for something to happen. They were told by the people in the small village they lived, that the day anyone buries their loved one, the spirit will come back that evening at exactly midnight and knock at their door, so no wonder that the children were silent in anticipation. There were no footsteps to be heard but a knock did come at exactly midnight, the two frightened children did not open the door to see who it was, they just waited for the knock to stop and go away, they knew that it would be the spirit of their departed mother and that they were not to open the door on any account. The silence which followed was deafening.

That night the little girl was too afraid to sleep in her own bed, she clung to her older brother, seeking not only reassurance but comfort and protection, so in the end he agreed that she will sleep in the same bed as him, holding her tight and telling her in his soft voice that everything will be alright. She sobbed quietly that night and finally when she managed to sleep she was to be awakened by a nightmare terrifying the small child beyond belief. She had been dreaming of an outrageously large maggot crawling across her small body and she had woken up screaming and crying her heart out. Her older brother did try his best to reassure her and to make her go back to sleep once again but not until he looked everywhere in the small bed for the maggot that the little child dreamed about and not until she was totally convinced that there was nothing there.

The next couple of weeks were going to be very busy in preparation for the coming of their father, who was going to take them to a town where he lived and worked. They had not seen him for almost four years, so they did not know what to expect and were not easy at the prospect of meeting him again and going back with him despite the fact that he was their father and that it was expected of him to take care of his children. There was lot to be done. There were no possessions to be taken care of but the children needed attention. The boy was so much older so there was very little to be done with him but the little girl was infested with lice and had nothing to wear. One of the neighbours began the task of clearing her small head of lice. The child sat for two whole days in their house with a towel wrapped around her head, some kind of powder in her hair which would hopefully kill the lice. She could not go out at all so she was amused by the resident red squirrel hopping everywhere, coming to see her and running away again. Two days and the lice were gone but not the eggs which still clung to the hair and had to be removed with a special comb or picked by hand. It was going to be a long process and it would have to be still carried on after the child returned with her father to the city. The dress was also made, the little girl delighted with it and thinking that it was the prettiest thing she had ever had. On a white background there were tiny little bunches of blue flowers with tiny little leaves looking like little bouquets. The dress was made to last so it was virtually to the floor, puff sleeves which could take two arms yet alone one slim one and a smocking at the top part which would stretch as she grew. Now there was nothing else to do but wait for their father to arrive.

He did finally arrive bringing with him with another man who they were told was their uncle. It all felt very strange and the meeting with the children, neighbours and family went well but the little girl would not go to her father, she sat in the corner of her bed looking frightened and bewildered, close to tears. Her uncle she did like, with his wrinkled kind face, she felt that it was alright to eventually come and sit on his knees and talk to him. He did have some sweeties and that might have helped to break the little child's fear and apprehension. They eventually were ready to leave but there was still one thing to attend too. The children had a dog living with them, their constant companion and a guardian of the little girl when she was left on her own while the mother was in hospital and the brother out. The beautiful Alsatian the little girl adored and did not want to leave behind so not only pleaded with her father and her uncle but she cried openly cuddling her faithful friend not wanting to let him go, not wanting to leave him behind with somebody else; but there was no other way as he could not come to the town or the flat that they would be living from now on. The dog was left with one of the neighbours on their farm leaving the child heart-broken, hating the adults for being so cruel, hating having to go somewhere unknown, unfamiliar, frightening. Finally the child exhausted from so much crying, with her brother holding her hand and her nice uncle comforting her, in total silence, began the short journey to the small station and the wait for the train to take them to the unknown new world to the town in which they were to live with their father, uncle and his wife and a cousin ill with tuberculosis, the illness which took their mother away. Even the cart trip drawn by horses which she would normally love so much did nothing to alleviate the child's misery. She did not want to go with her father, she would have much preferred to stay with her beautiful dog and the thoughts of living in an unknown town with people she did not know filled her with dread and apprehension.

The little house where the two children were at the time of their mother's death was not the only place they had lived. Their mother had come back to her roots, the place of her birth and the place where she had met and married the father of her children. Almost two years after the little girl was born she had left her husband realising that her marriage was over, that there was nothing else to do but to go home and take the children with her. The village was remotely situated in the south part of Poland, no more than a dozen dwellings making up the whole of the village. There were no such luxuries as running water, toilet, separate bedrooms, everyone lived in the same room, sometimes divided into two parts to create some kind of privacy. Families lived together, sharing the space available to them, having some privacy by putting a partition in the same room. Many a time beds were mattresses placed on the floor and filled with horsehair or straw. The comfort was provided by the duvets which were warm filled with goose down and so were the huge pillows. All the houses had big stoves in their corners providing the cooking facilities and heat needed.

The mother was born in the small village of Skarzysko-Kammienne and lived there and there she also met her husband. She was very striking with her pallid complexion blue eyes and jet-black hair which hung to her waist when it was unbraided and which she wore plaited and coiled on the nape of her neck. Her husband was also dark his eyes deep brown in contrast sporting a small moustache, slim and good looking. She was five years older then him but did not look it. They married and the first child was born in the village of Skarzysko-Kamienne a boy in the month of October of 1940. They lived there in the remote village until 1945. During the time the husband was called away to serve in the army during the war, not seeing his family, the war taking him all over the place, joining the French resistance and getting shot, the bullet just missing his chest and going through his left arm. The bullet penetrated his left arm leaving it withered, his fingers curled in such a way that he could not ever open them except for his thumb. The small shrapnel left there remain in his arm for the rest of his life. It was nothing as far as he was concerned, at least he came out of it with his life, when so many were lost. It did not stop him from coming back to his painting and decorating job, his right arm taking most of the load and the injured arm helping. On the return they decided that they would move to Gniezno where his mother lived and where he was born and also where his sister lived. His mother was widowed twice, losing her first husband during the First World War. The place where grandmother lived was big in comparison with the little house the children knew, it had a bedroom, living room which served also at night time as another bedroom, a kitchen and a toilet just outside in the corridor. The dark solid furniture was filled with china and glass and above the dresser there was a picture of a cavalryman in full uniform – her first husband. He was on a beautiful horse, elegant and erect very handsome indeed. Many years later when her grandmother and her aunt died she did try to get the picture, but nobody knew what has happened to it. Her grandmother's second husband died of an illness but she has never found out which. The move to the small town of Gniezno was practical as there would be more work for the father and they would be able after a while to get their own flat to live in. They did get their own flat outside the main town near the small forest where the mother was able to take her son for walks and teach him all about the different berries that grew there during the summer month and which you could eat safely and which you could not. In the autumn time you would go and find wild mushrooms, and the boy again would learn very quickly which were good and which you must not touch because they would poison you or give you blisters. He loved the forest, the freedom which provided and the many wonders that there were to be discovered. That need to be amongst the nature, the freedom which he felt there amongst the trees, the peace which he enjoyed so much stayed with him all of his life. They were happy there for some time to come, the father doing well in his work, and his wife looking after the boy and the flat, tending the small patch of vegetables outside their home. In 1949 another child was born a little girl in a month of May. She had very fine features, very dainty, almost doll-like. The was one more child born five years after the first but his infant death was surrounded by stories and mystery. She would hear about it from her grandmother when she was teenager. The tale told by her grandmother stayed with her all her life. She never did discover how much truth the story held. Much later in life when she mentioned the story to her brother he did not know anything about it.

The family remained in Gniezno until the little girl was about two years old and then the mother decided to leave her husband and go back to the village where she was born. There was nothing else to do but move, her husband not only working hard but drinking excessively, many a time coming home very drunk without his wage packet. The little girl remembering one such occasion when her father came home drunk bringing with him no money but some oranges. Her mother in sheer exasperation hurling the oranges at her father asking him how was she to feed the family. The husband began staying away from home having girlfriends here and there. He was a good-looking man so there was no shortage of willing females. The mother began getting very thin, not only from worries but from lack of nourishment, looking after the children first and thinking of herself last. When she finally returned to her home village she had already contracted tuberculosis.

In the small village in the south of Poland with its few dwellings and simple life a new chapter in their life would begin, ending with their beloved mother's death.

THE RED RUSTY GATE

Peter Breheny

Using my car I access a landscape from a secret place, wind down the window and breath in the clean refreshing air. I would like to walk across this landscape but I am unable to do so. Instead, using my eyes, my mind wonders from where I am.

In front of me a red rusty five bar gate, stops access to a field but not the view, beyond. The gate set between ancient limestone posts is secured at one end by a single strand of fencing wire and at the other an old chain held together with baling twine which secures it against trespass.

The field is surrounded by a dry-stone-wall constructed from thin flat pieces of limestone; growing over the surface of the wall are lichens of pale orange and white, some of the white lichen has a tinge of green.

The surrounding wall is old and has been repaired many times. Every nine or ten feet a fence post is positioned but not secured on either side. The pole is holding two strands of barbed wire. The wire runs along the wall top to stop sheep and cattle from climbing over it.

At present the field is empty of livestock. Here and there stunted prickly clumps of thistle grow to a height of only a few feet. In the far right corner of the field a bed of stingy nettles surrounds a rotting heap of farm yard manure, feeding off it. Later in the year the manure will be spread to nourish the field.

Yellow buttercups live here in abundance and beyond my chosen field other fields slope down into the valley, some empty like the one in front of me. Others, with flocks of sheep busily grazing, building up body and fleece ready for the winter snows.

To my left on the other side of the valley the prominent shape of Ecton Hill stands proud, concealing a labyrinth of tunnels from where lead and silver has been mined since before Roman times.

Closer, smaller hills crowned with spinneys of Ash and smaller solitary Hawthorns are dotted along dry-stone-walls. In the far and distance haze other hills place themselves between this valley and the next, beyond which, I know sits Buxton hidden from view with its ancient Roman Spa.

A grey overcast sky threatens thunder, when suddenly in the foreground a gangly hare, lopes along the track pursued by a stoat, both seemingly oblivious to my presence. Death is close and in my mind's eye, I see him crossing the ancient landscape a thousand times.

100 Word Stories

REVIEWING

Harry Wilson

Reviewing my old school reports, I noticed my English teacher commented "has acting ability" that after being cast as Ebenezer Scrooge in Dickens' 'A Christmas Carol'.

A few years later, I joined The People's Theatre, Newcastle and played Ferdinand in The Tempest opposite Miranda.

In a forest scene looking for logs, I picked up a heavy limb, took the strain hoisting it onto my shoulder. On the last performance the cast, playing a trick, made a realistic log of balsa wood. Bending, taking the strain, it shot over my shoulder, over the footlights, just missing the first row of audience!

ENTERING THE HALLWAY OF THE NURSING HOME

Vikki Fitt

Entering the hallway of the nursing home, my nostrils are assaulted by the familiar mixture of incontinence, ineffectual air freshener and school dinners.

I proceed, past the jovial, bustling carers, to the tropical climes of the conservatory. My once-beautiful, beloved Mum slumps sleepily in her wing chair, wig askew, stripy socks like Pippi Longstocking's protecting the fragile flesh of her matchstick legs, her beloved teddy clutched to her chest.

"Yoohoo," I call gently; she jerks awake, her rheumy eyes unseeing but her face slowly lighting up in a gap-toothed smile as she recognises, from long ago, the call of 'family'.

SIMON

Harry Wilson

Simon, young Australian, hiking in Derbyshire, called to a young girl Zara, working in a garden, "Would you please fill my water bottle?" "Come in." Simon stayed for the rest of the day and welcomed for the next four weeks.

Zara was smitten and when Simon suggested she might like to visit his parents in Sydney, she agreed paying both Quantas fares.

Reaching London, Simon advised he would check Quantas tickets, she to stay in the waiting room. Two hours later, panicking, Zara decided to call the airline to be told Simon had taxied to Heathrow taking an earlier flight.

VISIT TO BELFAST

Peter Breheny

In a gesture of friendship to a fellow writer he'd placed his hand on my shoulder as he left the bar. Over a few pints of Guinness we'd discussed his book in the company of another volunteer, also a writer. Out of politeness I'd ignored the act that had brought him to public notoriety, the alleged killing of five people and the injuries inflicted on 31 others. An operation that had failed because she had walked away from the rubble, later, he'd publicly stated regret that anybody had to lose their lives. I had liked him, admiring his excellent book.

ALISON

Harry Wilson

Alison, at teacher training college, Durham, had the misfortune to 'lose' her spectacles not once but three times, her mother reluctantly paying out £150 each time.

Years later, surprised, Alison received a long anonymous letter from a college acquaintance. "I was jealous, you were attractive, especially wearing glasses, popular and I stole them, my conscience will not allow me to stay silent – I'm so sorry!!"

Later that year, Christmas Eve, there was a knock on Alison's door, when answered revealed Chrissie, her college acquaintance. "I just have to apologise personally and recompense your loss – please accept my cheque for £450."

YELLOW PAINT MINI-SAGA

Vikki Fitt

Twilit November murk. Drive to Homebase after draining day feigning control of bolshy infants. Aim: to relieve SAD symptoms by purchasing five litres of life-enhancing, sunflower yellow emulsion, transforming gloomy, sunless kitchen into glowing haven. Ignore piddling safety advice, jam tin behind driver's seat, merge into rush-hour queue grinding slowly downhill to grid-locked roundabout. Hear barely perceptible clonk. Tentatively probe behind seat, heart plummets, hand reappears dripping vivid yellow. Clutches gearstick (yellow), then steering-wheel (yellow), whilst unstoppable sunflower tsunami envelops shoes and pedals. Yellow hand and white face press against misty window in silent Munchian scream. SAD has become sadder.

A Shooting Visit

THE GUN PLACE

Janis Clark

It was hidden away, The Gun Place
Deep in a rural space
The tangles at the gate and the peeping sign
Hardly spoke to the visitor
This way's fine
Because it's not!
Not for the casual passer-by or
The crooked criminal in pursuit of material gain
He cannot be bothered to earn
They are the 'uninvited'.

We, the privileged few
Our way found
Just.
Up the track we wound
As did Mrs de Winter at Manderley, after the wilderness took over
A dead place, full of its own life
In an other-worldly way

Around a bend, and another, we found the gun place
Long and low, crouching, with its back to us
Did we believe in what we were doing?
Not really
Guns are not for us
They can kill indiscriminately
Why are we here?
Curiosity

Inside, our implacability is worn down a little
Kind men who handle lethal weapons
Offer us tea
We wait for all to gather
Two by two, as in the ark, they came
And we are spoken to, given instruction

The friends of our friend are allotted
Guns
We pick them up. Load them. Fire
At targets some yards off
My instructor has gentle brown eyes
Belying his calling as 'ARMED RESPONSE OFFICER'
His voice is gentle too
He is calm. Patient
The sort of policeman I remember of old
Who would make you feel safe

I am no competitor
I have no wish to win
And I don't
But I am glad for the experience
Glad to feel that sensible men, in the main
Are in charge of guns

HOW SHOOTING CHANGED MY LIFE

Peter Breheny

Until recently helping meant just talking
The Refuge for Battered Wives had always taken up a lot of my time
Trying to understand
A friendly shoulder to cry on
Until recently I couldn't really offer much more
But the women said it helped
Even though I always came away wishing I could offer more
Writing was how I relaxed
We met at Peter's house on the first Saturday of each month
Read our work to each other
It was a day I looked forward to
The bus ride
Through the countryside
Ashbourne
The conversation the tea the socialising
Then Pete had suggested a visit to his shooting club
Something different for all of you he said, you'll enjoy it
Would I, I wondered?
It turned out only the two Peter's and Bill had ever fired a rifle before
For myself, Annie, Doreen, Jan, Moy, Nat and Rachael it was to
be a new experience
Some of us were reluctant, because guns have one purpose, to kill
You'll enjoy it Peter kept telling us
We don't shoot people and we don't shoot animals – just paper targets
Oh what the hell, I'll give it a go
But once there I chickened out
It was something my daughter had said to me
She'd asked if someone like me in my late 70s should be
endangering myself in this way?
They all talked about the kick
I had visions of the kick breaking my shoulder

Don't think I'll shoot, perhaps I'll just watch
Yes you will shoot – said Mike Sparkes, the gentleman Peter had arranged to be my minder for the day
There's no pulling out now, it's too late for that
I'll look after you Pat, came his commanding voice
You'll be OK with me, come along now Pat, just follow my instructions
I followed him out to the shooting point
Mike showed me the tiny .22 bullets we'd be shooting.
You'll feel nothing, I promise
I did as instructed.
Donning first the ear muffs then the safety glasses
I was given fifty bullets, forty to practice with the last ten to be saved for the competition.
Mike took me through a series of breathing exercises
Showed me how to hold the rifle properly
Which part of the target to aim at
How to squeeze, the trigger
My first five bullets all struck the black.
Not bad said Mike, not bad at all
His strong hands sent a tingle down my back as he moulded my shoulders, my back and my head into position for the next five shots
Please excuse my hands said Mike, we've got to get you into the correct position.
That's quite alright Mike, I said with a grin
Whatever it was he did to me seemed to work, I scored four 10s and a 9.
Bloody hell, said Mike, I think I might have a budding marikswoman on my hands
My next five shots were all 10s, all bulls eyes
Mike was gob-smacked; I can't believe it he said
Are you sure you've never fired a rifle before?
I felt pleased with myself
Fired another five shots, scoring ten bulls
Bloody hell, said Mike, again, that's amazing
Does that mean I might be a natural killer, I asked laughingly

I don't know about that Pat, but you're a natural shooter.
To my own amazement and everyone else's, I won the competition with a maximum score of 100.
Nigel the club chairman presented me with a little glass tankard, commenting that my score really deserved something much grander.
In the heat of the moment they asked me to join the club as a full member, which I did
After months of one-to-one training I applied for a Fire Arms Certificate and now have my own rifle.
In a quiet very private sort of way, I've become a lot more positive with my work at the Refuge for Battered Wives
Far less women are signing in these days
I've even been awarded an MBE for services to women
'I do admire the work you're doing,' said the Queen
If only she knew the half of it.

SNIPER

Nathanael Ravenlock

The announcement came in just after sunrise – the Prophet had been located.

Within the hour I was in the chopper with the doors slid open, flying through the morning air. The briefing had been short and sharp. We all knew what to do, we had planned for years, drilled for months, waiting for this precise moment. The briefing was protocol. Our mission had to be documented precisely. We had to prove everything had been done correctly and legally.

Before stepping aboard the chopper, the commander steered me, by the elbow, out of earshot of the rest of the crew.

"I don't need to tell you how important this is, do I?"

"No, sir." I replied.

"You're the best shooter we have – that's why I requested you personally. You've got one shot," he reminded me, emphasising it by holding up his index finger. "One shot! Make it true! Make it count! Make it the best damn shot of your life!"

"Yes, sir." I nodded.

"You know how long we've waited to get this close to him?! When he's out of range he damn well vanishes like a ghost. It takes years, years! to find him again." The commander looked me straight in the eye then spoke softly. "The world waits!"

He patted me on the shoulder and shoved me toward the chopper. He barked some commands at the gathered crew and we all boarded.

The gritted wind cut into my face and bought me back to the now.

I looked around at the crew, made up from people from all over the world, drafted in for this single mission. It was a mission which deeply interested the world, for the future depended on it. There would be a future if we failed, but it would be a future in which we failed.

This wasn't my first mission. I'd fired my rifle thousands of times on the practice range and hundreds of times in the field. I'd been to dozens of war-torn countries and never missed my mark. But this was different, somehow more difficult because I had one single shot and all depended on it.

"We have a visual!" The tracker's voice whipped through my eardrum, propelled from my headphones. "He's heard the 'copter! He's on the run!"

I leaned out of the open doorway and on the horizon I could just make out movement – he was travelling quickly.

"We need to get lower!" I shouted into the microphone, and the chopper descended.

As we closed, I raised the rifle to my shoulder and put my eye against the sight.

All went quiet. It was not true silence, for there was noise all around me, but I heard none of it. A whisper swam across my mind.

"Take a deep breath as you aim." It said, with the voice of my range master. His words had never left me in all the years I had uscd a gun.

I lined the figure up with the cross-hairs but the chopper was unsteady in the wind and the target never seemed to be in the same place for more than a nanosecond.

"There's a storm closing in quickly! We need to finish this! Now!" The commander's voice cut through the silence.

"I need to be lower!" I shouted, "And hold it steady!"

The chopper slid down, sending dust plumming upwards. The target was lost momentarily in a golden mist.

I felt the rhythm of the chopper, the pumping of my heart. I took a deep breath and felt my pulse slow. I cloaked myself in an aura of calm and waited. Then suddenly, through a gap in the dust cloud, I could see his shape once more – a shadow on the desert floor.

I moved with the rhythm of the chopper, the point at which I aimed got tighter and tighter until it spun on a pinhead. I placed my index finger on the trigger and felt its reassuring resistance. I let out my breath and squeezed.

The pilot pulled up and the air cleared. We circled around as the dust settled. There lay the body of the Prophet.

We landed close-by and the crew dived out of the chopper to secure the area. With my job done, theirs now began. I calmly packed away the rifle and climbed out after them.

I walked over to where the body of the Prophet lay – silent and majestic.

I knelt next to him – he looked so proud, so serene. He was a leader who saw the world as it should be. I placed my hand upon his chest as the crew hurried around me, doing their duties – removing the tracking device, extracting rich royal blood, measuring his gigantic Imperial tusks.

A smile played across my face as I looked at the tranquilliser dart protruding from the Prophet's wrinkled pelt. Beneath my hand I felt his slow, steady breath as he slumbered.

Soon the sedative would wear off and he would awake. I would never again have the opportunity to bask in his overwhelming presence. For in him lay the answers, for he is the Prophet, the last of the great white elephants.

THE MUSKETEER

Annie Noble

Firing a musket – three words.
They tell me nothing.
An image – dry as dust.
Men wearing white trousers, uniform jackets, black hat, black boots.

Firing a musket.
Bang
Smoke
That's all.

My world turned on its axis.

A musket
Smooth, brown-grained wood
Long
Almost as long as I am tall
The weight – heavy and unwieldy
A good arm-stretch, butt pushed into shoulder
The flint – a real flint – dark grey-
Scalloped edges – pointed at one end –
Striking end banging down on metal,

Making sparks
For the black powder
Tipped in the flash pan

Main charge tipped down the muzzle
Followed by the lead bullet
Bigger than a marble
Resting on its patch –
The difference between smooth flight
Or "rattle and roll"
Ramrod pushing it all home.

Raising the gun and taking aim
A joke!
Point it at the target – approximately – and hope.

Trigger at half-cock . . .

Suspense. . .

I don't know what to expect . . .

Adrenalin . . .

FIRE!

More suspense . . .

Thirty seconds of suspense . . .

Waiting . . .

Spark's journey time from flash pan to charge . . .

Nothing.

Re-charge the flash pan . . .

Repeat . . .

Suspense . . .

Nothing.

Repeat . . .

Suspense . . .

BANG

Barreljoltsintoshoulderpuffofsmokefrom
panheatonhandfirefrommuzzlesmoke
hanginginairsmellofsulphur

WOW!

Like going down an almost vertical water slide
So fast there's not even time to say "Bloody hell" before hitting bottom.

Legs shake . . .
Firing a musket once . . .
Suspense . . .
Noiseheatsmokefiresmellpain

Firing a musket in battle.
Up all night making cartridges
Loading the box
Kill or be killed
Fear writhing in guts
Is it life or death today?

Six hundred muskets
Two hundred in the hands of kneeling men
Two hundred more behind
In the hands of standing men
And another two hundred behind for backup
God knows what they might do

Hand us spares
Or shoot our heads off.

Kneeling on the grass
White trousers stained green
And maybe brown
Or red.

Prime! Load! Make ready! Fire!

Prime ! Load! Make ready! Fire!
Prime load make ready fire
Primeloadmakereadyfire
Heatfiresmokesmell

Screams

Burning-deafening-smoke hanging in still air-stench

So thick we can't see who we're firing at
Can't see whether they are falling, advancing, retreating

Can't see can't hear can't think
Daren't think.

Prime! Load! Make ready! Fire!

All I know is I'm still standing

Prime! Load! Make ready! Fire!

Shit!
The smoke's clearing . . .
They're nearly on us . . .

Primeloadmakereadyfireprimeloadmakereadyfireprimeloadmaker
eadyfire

Get 'em up get'em up Get 'em up get'em up Get 'em up get'em
up

Primeloadmakereadyfire!

Bayonets out!

CHARGE . . .

AT THE GUN CLUB

Patricia Ashman

Rigid with attention
I concentrate on every word
Safety is in the detail
Focus, look at it
As close as this
I am distracted by the beauty
Of polished wood,
matt black metal
An inanimate object
full of silent menace
Because we all know
what it could do
A thing of beauty
and craftsmanship
can be ugly
in the hands of a human being
Flint arrowheads,
patiently, lovingly
chipped and shaped

Death to bison and deer
Flashing metal blades,
dripping bloody edges,
ruby red filling the grooves
of delicate engraving
When such is their purpose,
They shouldn't be beautiful
Cumbersome muskets,
fussy to load,
wildly random,
bang, flash, smokescreen
All together lads,
Step up… Fire…
Soldiers are…
Replaceable

But this is Sport,
and I clear my mind
as I handle a gun
for the first time

Later, Ask me,
Is it very satisfying
to hit the target?
I'm afraid it is

Sculpture

OUR VISIT TO THE SCULPTOR SIMON MANBY – 2 JUNE 2012

Peter Breheny

We arrive at 11.30am after a drive through the back lanes which brings us down from the Weaver Hills into the village of Wootton. Simon meets us at the gate, pulling my wheelchair across the paddock. The paddock all decked out in red, blue and white bunting ready for the village Jubilee celebration tomorrow. We entered the old barn, now Simon's studio, by the back door to save negotiating the front steps. Nat, Rachael, Peter, Harry and Josie are already waiting, having made their own introductions. We are followed in by Jan, who's made a few accidental detours on route. I'm surprised to see Jan because she'd seemed unsure about wanting to join us this time and I couldn't think why.

A circle of chairs have been laid out ready for us amongst the exhibits, we'd hoped to sit in the garden but it's cold and wet. Lee's paintings adorn the white walls but she's nowhere to be seen. Amongst her paintings are a few drawings I recognise as Simons and all around on white plinths wonderful pieces of his sculpture. Carvings in stone and castings in bronze, most of the figures are female, none are clothed, they stand, recline and float in a variety of positions. I've always experienced a feeling of being in a sacred place when entering a gallery full of nude figures, it's the same feeling I get when I enter a church. The figures demand respect and quietude. Seeing these figures today, reminds me of visit made years ago with my infant son Paul. Paul would look around at the nudity then with a pointing finger, directed accusingly at Simon, repeating the words 'naughty, naughty.'

Simon positions me in the circle with my back hard against the wall, to my right a bronze bust of Jean-Jacques Rousseau about whom Simon has recently written a small book which is based on the Swiss-born philosopher's visit to Wootton Hall in 1766. The Bronze created by Simon two years ago is life size, I'd love to own it, but with a price tag of £3500 it's out of my price range, but I am the proud owner of a couple of Simon's drawings.

Eventually when everyone is seated I ask Simon to outline his career for my friends – trained at the Edinburgh School of Art where he met and married Lee. Simon's first job was lecturing at Stoke-on-Trent School of Art where he quickly became disillusioned with teaching and took the massive step of becoming a freelance sculptor. Simon seemed a little reticent to talk about himself, so I tried to help by asking questions that I already knew the answers to and to which I thought my friends might find interesting. Both Simon's parents had been artistic, his father an architect his mother, whom I remembered meeting on several occasions was the artist Judith Da Fano; a successful painter. His grandmother, Dorothea Sophia Zellner also a painter had been one of the lesser known Pre-Raphaelites. Only a few weeks earlier Simon had been contacted by a curator from one of the Paris museums who was writing a book about Augustine Rodin's Women. The curator had discovered a collection of letters from Dorothea written to Rodin when she was a young woman. A relationship, Simon and his family had been totally unaware of.

I'd always enjoyed and admired Simon's work and hoped my friends would too, but as the talk progressed and people asked questions I was surprised at just how full of self-doubt Simon was about his work. I'd always looked upon him as a great success, but I suppose if we're honest, we all have doubts about our own abilities, I know I do, especially when I'm writing, a process I sometimes find quite painful.

It was soon time for lunch. We unpacked our sandwiches and were served tea and coffee by Jo and her mother Lee. For a moment Louie, Jo's four-year-son, peeped in from the doorway but quickly disappeared back into the safety of the house when he realised he'd been spotted by this strange group of people. We relaxed and in the absence of a table, the various display plinths became resting places for our food and drink and it wasn't long before several reclining figures were being photographed by Rachael, as her photographic eye recognised the inappropriate and interesting placing of half-eaten sandwiches and drinks.

When lunch was finished and the rain had stopped, Simon suggested the group might like to stroll around the garden where they could view some larger pieces of his sculpture. While this was going on Nat and Simon pushed my wheelchair through into the stone carving shed, which had once been the old cow shed. Perched precariously on a tall stool in an effort to achieve the correct angle of fire, I attempted peeing into the folding rubber bladder that I'd brought along for just such an emergency. Having a pee can be a major problem to a wheelchair user when no proper disabled facilities are available. So be warned and aware of this when inviting a disabled person to your home. For your guidance, should you need it, the NHS produce an excellent publication called 'Peeing in public' it tells you, the host, all you need to know on the subject.

Nat and Simon chatted while I sorted myself out. In the middle of the room I notice a large object covered by a dust sheet. 'What's this,' I asked Simon? 'Nothing special,' he exclaimed nervously. 'Just something I'm working on for the Summer Exhibition. Be careful you don't catch it with your wheelchair Pete, it's a bit delicate.'

Back in the studio we settled down to more questions which came easier now people were relaxed. Rachael asked Simon how he first became interested in becoming a sculptor. Simon related how as a small boy he had been taken to visit the studio of the sculptress Margaret Wrightson, a friend of his mothers. He was so impressed that from that day on he too wanted to be a sculptor. Harry asked how an artist worked out how much to charge for his work, a difficult question. 'You get what you can' was Simon's answer. 'But it never seems to cover the number of hours spent, the cost of the bronze and the casting are a key factor, of course.' Doreen asked how he went about finding his models and was interested to know who they were? Simon explained that some were friends, some sitters at the local life class and on the odd occasion women he met would simply offer their services. For some it was a fantasy fulfilled, but always a private affair; Doreen dug deeper, asking more personal questions about the relationship between artist and model – Simon explained that for him, the act of carving or modelling the female figure was an act of love without being promiscuous.

As we spoke I noticed that Jan whose husband is also an artist asked no questions, unusual for Jan who usually has lots of questions, maybe she's bored, I thought. Nat asked why so many pieces depicted a female with a child? 'I'm not sure, I suppose I've always imagined these pieces as representing myself and my own mother. It's an image I have in my mind when I'm working.'

Eventually after two and a half hours we ran out of questions and came to a natural finish. We packed away our note pads offered our thanks to Simon and began to depart. Whilst all the others left by the front door, Simon and Nat made to take me out the back door, across the paddock to miss the steps at the front. Passing through the stone carving shed the front wheels of my wheelchair caught in an old drainage channel cut into the concrete floor, as a result my wheelchair shot off to the right. 'Watch out.' Shouted Simon, but it was too late, I'd bumped the piece of work covered by the dustsheet, which tottered momentarily – before I managed to steady it with my right hand, but in doing so, I'd snagged the dust sheet, which fell to the floor, exposing a life sized clay model of Jan our fellow writer in all her natural glory.

THE STATUE OF DAVID

Janis Clark

David gazed at the statue in awe. The beauty of the piece. The magnificence! A nude reclining, hand behind head, one knee bent. She looked, what was it? Happy? No. Fulfilled. Sensually struck. She had been all consumed and was drowsy with sex.

David was transfixed with the realness of her as if some tiny, living person dwelt within that bronze frame – her mood captured for eternity. The moment must have been ecstatic for her.

His thoughts moved on. Who was she? And why did she have that look? Was she the sculptor's lover? His wife? Or just someone in his imagination? Maybe someone he had wanted who was out of reach?

David reflected on his own wife. She was beautiful too. But how long was it since he'd seen *her* unclothed? He tried to think and then with a tug of panic, realised he could no longer recall every inch of her. Did she ever have the look of this woman? Her soft eyes maybe. And those sensuous lips. He mused more on womankind and her shape. They were all the same, yet different. The personality was where it really showed. Some kind, motherly, just a little subservient (his preference) and those, like his wife, sharp witted, career minded, clever.

He had loved this once. That is, until she became hardened and impatient with him. She moved on and up her career ladder, whereas, he was content to potter along, safe in his own orbit of expertise. Admittedly, working for an insurance company wasn't a job to excite the senses, but it was steady and sure.

She, on the other hand, was an intellectual. Or had become one. Forever studying. A late degree was in The Classics – her speciality, the Greek Myths. She had been so enthusiastic, regaling him with regular monotony on this or that character. In particular, Zeus, the all powerful God who could invoke havoc-ridden storms, yet loved many a woman. Leda was her favourite – she found her intriguing. How could she have fallen for a 'swan'? They were beautiful creatures to be sure, but why did Zeus hide himself as a swan in the first place? She had her own Freudian theories about this but scholars were divided.

'All rubbish', thought David.

But she had become passionate, ardent. He, in turn, became increasingly bored with the whole business and changed the subject whenever he could. Realising this, she talked less and less about her passion and eventually gave up altogether. He'd hardly noticed until she began to go out. It started with the old university pals creating a discussion group. Just once a month initially, then fortnightly. He realised something was up when it became more than once a week and suspicion crept in. He quizzed her a little. Where were the meetings? Who was there? That sort of thing. She enlightened him in a cheery, 'nothing to hide' sort of way but he wasn't totally reassured. Apparently, outsiders with an interest in the classics were permitted to join. She told him about the young student in her final year, the tutor who had a soft spot for mature students and who had taught them, and the artist who was inspired by the myths as so many had been before.

Looking at the bronze again, he thought to himself that the longer he looked, the more she reminded him of his wife. The hair was longer and more reminiscent of her younger days and the body was definitely youthful. But it was the toes! Those big toes that turned up, causing her shoes to have a short life as they wore away the soft leather with constant rubbing. They used to laugh about them, calling them her 'Hobbit toes'.

He reached out to touch them just the sculptor came in to his gallery. He smiled at David benignly, understanding the tactile properties of his work. David smiled back sheepishly and gave a little shrug. He turned to have one last glance before leaving, the smile still playing on his lips. Then his smile froze and he bent closer, This beauty was holding something. A feather.

'That's a swan's feather' said the sculptor helpfully.

Lowry

LOWRY'S WORK

Jo Manby

Upstairs, a selection of Lowrys hung against picture gallery red walls combining drawings with oils and generous quantities of information to assist the visitor in interpreting the work. The Man with Red Eyes (1936); the Portrait of Ann (1957); the pair, Little Girl Seen from the Front and Little Girl Seen from the Back, both from 1964. Five Office Portraits in pencil. The limited palette. The rough worked canvases and boards – Lowry painted with his fingers as well as his brushes.

His isolation comes through as if the walls were breathing loneliness, the sea whispering of immensity and the landscapes of emptiness. Expressions of these emotions can be traced on people's faces in his portraits and pictures. Even in Going to the Match, where the figures are like tiny sticks, people are driven to their entertainment, a mass of singular individuals. These works show his concept of society – he felt he was outside it, observing; but he also acknowledged he could easily be any one of these people. The power of Lowry's work to speak to an audience of aspects of their own shared humanity emerges – their emotions and experiences. His job as a rent collector gave him an insight into the domestic, financial and social world of the Salford and Manchester working class.

Lowry's work doesn't appeal on an immediately aesthetic level, like the Impressionists or the Fauves, but appeals to the human spirit. One can feel the grit of the white roads, wet with rain, reflecting the wan sunlight; smell the damp overcoats and the smoky chimneys, the soot in the air.

There was something dogged about the way he restricted himself to four colours and black and white, and the same few themes, it was categorically 'work' for him; it was also a compulsion. He banished nature from the urban landscape; the only place it appears is as strictly controlled elements in parks and as a green tinge to land- and cityscapes. An example of the combining of drawing and oil painting was shown the day we visited in the juxtaposition of drawings of Peel Park, Salford, and the painting which these drawings led to, illustrating how Lowry manoeuvred his way round a composition, with the building blocks of hedges and trees and flower beds having the same pictorial weight as the buildings and the flight of steps themselves.

LOWRY

Vikki Fitt

Saltburn seascape, flake white stretching into infinity,
Textured oils broken by the blackened hulk of a smoke-stacked coaster.
Remote rural landscapes with rounded curves,
Reminiscent of full-bodied feminine forms,
In stark contrast to the angular planes of Lancashire's urban streets.

The mills and factories, the rundown terraces, the town hall,
All rendered in a trademark palette
Of black and white, of Prussian blue, vermilion and ochre.
Throngs gather and bustle about their business:
the 'matchstick men', the grotesques.
"Everyone is a stranger to everyone else. All my people are lonely",
the artist declared. "Crowds are the most lonely thing of all."

Bleakest of all, the bedroom,
Black brass bed spread with snowy counterpane,
A dark, dismal and dreary shrine to his invalid mother,
Domineering and disappointed,
A photographic negative of Van Gogh's bright, sunlit room.

In that same Pendlebury house lay his own monastic cell,
The one indulgence of his long, solitary life,
Rossetti's alluring pre-Raphaelites lining the walls,
Companions for the dying artist, surrounding his celibate bed
Like a host of erotic angels.

THE LOWRY VISIT

Jo Manby

Harry Goodwin's's[3] monochrome photography was hung along the length of the Promenade Gallery at The Lowry the day we visited in May, featuring 1960s stars – The Supremes, The Beach Boys, The Zombies, Jimi Hendrix, Little Richard, Elton John – some were taken at the BBC Studios on Dickenson Road in Longsight, just around the corner from where I used to live when I worked at The Lowry. It was good to see Harry's work on display at The Lowry, since when I worked there I met him and admired his photographs.

I tried to visualise how it all began, The Lowry. It was still a building site when I started working there in 2000. The surrounding land was a sea of ploughed up mud, occupied by JCBs and men in hard hats. A tiny cabin, the works canteen, where I used to go for lunch sometimes with my colleagues, served thickly-cut chips. There was no Lowry Outlet Mall and no Imperial War Museum North until a couple of years later.

Then apartment blocks started going up, and there was the bidding war for the BBC in the North, whether it would stay in Manchester or decamp to Salford. The Professional Footballers' Association paid £1.9 million for Going to the Match. The values of all the other Lowrys then shot up in unison. People came in droves to identification sessions where staff had to tell people that they were

[3] Harry Goodwin, photographer: born Rusholme, Manchester 21 July 1924, died Manchester 23 September 2013.

in the business of identifying not valuing, and refer them on as necessary to the local branches of the leading fine art auction houses.

Many contemporary artists showed at The Lowry over the years. The first show was called The Double, taking its lead from Lowry's interest in twins as a phenomenon that sparked his creative impulse. Alice Maher drew a fountain of long black hair in charcoal directly onto the gallery wall. It was decried as a mockery of more traditional art but by the end of the exhibition, when it was due to be painted over with standard gallery white, there was uproar. Natasha Kidd in a later show exhibited a white paint plumbing system or 'painting machine', the specially commissioned Flow and Return, that pumped emulsion round the top floor gallery (The Deck) and had it dripping out into runnels and gutters before being recycled and pumped round again. Tracy Emin's neon work was featured; young Mancunian artists such as Liam Spencer and Martin Murray exhibited; and a group show, Thermo 03, was developed bringing together Manchester and Salford artists and art graduates.

When I started at The Lowry I was one of three Assistant Curators. One of the perks of the job included writing briefing notes about the galleries for staff in preparation for The Queen's visit. I was also a companion to a private collector of Futurist art from Lampedusa, Italy, and to the leading Indian artist Bhupen Khakhar on his visit and residency at The Lowry. Tasks included ordering watercolour paints for him and making sure he got back to his hotel safely in the evening.

All three of us were project managing major exhibitions and meeting all sorts of influential people. One job we split between us, and always enjoyed, was the interviewing of famous people alongside their favourite Lowry. I interviewed, among others, Andrew Motion, Johnny Ball and Roger McGough. We had a great job there, facilitating the public's enjoyment and understanding, not only of L S Lowry's increasingly well-respected oeuvre, but of modern and contemporary art more generally.

LOWRY: I DISLIKE

Nathanael Ravenlock

Staring at blank canvas
and that's what I see:
People flocking to mills –
Don't paint them with glee.

Each one a stranger
to all those around.
Most lonely of all things,
that creature, the Crowd.

I dislike them myself:
The men of the stick,
the people-milling crowds,
I'm just stick of it.

They don't really exist,
I have to confess,
they're just an expression
of my loneliness.

LOWRY: ON ART

Nathanael Ravenlock

Paint from your mind's eye,
it gets nearer to true.
With just a blank canvas,
no facts hamper you.

THE LOWRY SAGA

Peter Breheny

Who wants to come?
Put my name down
I'll come
Book the bus
It'll be fun

12 seats sold
To Uni Writers and friends
£10.51 each
Months before
That's it then

On the day it's
Moy & Annie, Pete & Paul,
Henryka & David,
Harry, Jenny & Harold,
Sarah & Margaret and Janet

The journey progresses
Uncomfortable seats
Bounce me about
Throwing me forward
Pain grips my backside

The journey boring
Through Stockport
Traffic crawling
The same pedestrians
Overtaking us

Mums with prams
A man on crutches
A dog with a bone
Ice cones with children
A cyclist with a death wish

At the lights
We shudder
We stop
We start
We brake, we're late

At last we turn left
The motorway beckons
But the driver's lost
Up a dead end
On industrial estate

We moan
We grown
The driver's a pain
Like the one in my backside
Frustration growing

We hit the motorway
A cheer goes up
We gain speed
Constant velocity is achieved
Relieving buttock pain

Two more wrong turns
Before the right one
Arriving at Salford Quays
The driver is friendless
Jenny the cake lady beats him verbally

We are met in reception by
Jo and her boy Louie and
Vikki the Fitt
Nat, Rachael and baby Reuben
Nowhere to be seen

We go our separate ways
We, to the bar
Me, for gin and tonic
Soon we are joined by others
All complaining about the driver

We tour the galleries
In my wheelchair
Paul pushing
Mary McCartney's
Pictures catch my eye

Tracey Emin as
Mexican artist
Frida Khalo
Marianne Faithful
With Madonna's head

Vivienne Westwood
With grey hat
Heavy red lipstick
Heavy eye make-up
Wrinkled face

We stare and glare
An image of Helen Mirren
XX tattooed on left thumb
Tender wrinkles around sensual eyes
Memories of Cal

Dowager Duchess of Devonshire
A brilliant sense of humour they claim
Frumpy blue dress
Matching umbrella
Attended by concrete dog

Behind the scenes
In the dressing room
The dancers of the Royal Ballet
Relax, ignoring the camera
Boobs on view

Lowry drawings
Girl with no shoulders
Horrible heads
Landscapes real and imaginary
Berwick –on- Tweed

A simple man
Who used simple colours
Ivory black, Vermillion,
Prussian blue, Yellow ochre
And Flake white

They say, Lowry said
You don't need brains to be a painter
Just feelings
I'm not an artist
I'm a man who paints

Scenes of industrial life
A sign invites us to draw on a postcard
Paul stands his on a Lowry
Photographs it with his mobile
It's removed by the curator

Lowry was born in 1887
A fire watcher in the second war
And an official war artist
Age 27 when the first war started
I find no record of his service?

Secretive and mischievous
A depressive man
Had several lady-friends
But at 88 claimed to be a virgin
Painted erotic works in secret

Seen as a failure by his mother
Lowry a shy man who once said
Had I not been lonely
None of my work
Would have happened

Rejected by the London establishment
They bought his work
Refusing to display it
Stored it in dark places
Until Tate Modern honoured him

Twice he declined an OBE
And once a CBE
Even a knighthood
And twice the Companion of Honour
Does Lowry hold the record for rejecting honours?

After we'd toured the gallery
I met up with Louie and Jo
Louie held the modern equivalent
Of a match-stick man from the gift shop
A Bendy man made from rubber

I buy two
One each for Hannah and Kaiya
They love them
Kaiya especially entwines the two
Innocently into erotic positions

We leave at five
Saying goodbye to those
Who'd come by car and tram
The ride back as uncomfortable
As the ride out

Annie collects the coach money
A week later I receive the invoice
Asking for £40 more than quoted
I post a cheque
Saying I'll pay no more

Introducing The Uni Writers

The group was originally set up in August 2006 by Peter Breheny and Annie Noble after graduating from the University of Derby, where their principle lecturers were Moy McCrory, Simon Heywood, the late Jerry Hope, and Carl Tighe. The idea was to encourage the act of creative writing by establishing and keeping in contact with other writers, as well as sharing work and experiences. The Uni Writers now has a committed membership of twelve – our youngest member being 30 and our oldest in his early 90s. Our gatherings are enjoyable events at which our work is read and constructive feedback given within a friendly atmosphere. The group meet at Channel House in Ashbourne on the first Saturday of every month. We are always happy to welcome new writers, whatever their ability and interests.

Patricia Ashman – Derbyshire born; school; work; marriage; three daughters; moved to Rugby; St. Paul's College Teacher Training; teaching in Rugby; teaching in Derbyshire; retirement; travelling; accumulated nine grandchildren and two great-grandchildren.

Peter Breheny – trained as a graphic designer and photographer at both the Salford and Manchester Schools of Art and Design where he gained a Dip AD before spending a career in advertising. Upon retirement he attended the University of Derby gaining a BA (Hon) degree in Creative Writing. He is at present researching Troubles literature for his doctorate.

Janis Clark has been writing for over thirty years with published works being freelance newspaper and magazine articles. In 2003, she began a full time degree in Creative Writing at The University of Derby. Having worked for many years as a film and television supporting artiste (extra), her aim was to write screen plays. She was soon enlightened to the fact that at least 10,000 others had the same wish and only one would be accepted!

However, she has written short stories and poetry and is enjoying the pursuit of this aspect of her literary career.

Vikki Fitt is in the process of taking phased retirement after decades of hard labour slogging away at the educational coalface. She is relishing the opportunities that are springing up with more available time, not least to have the opportunity to write. She has travelled widely and raised a family, which has been a regular source of inspiration. Vikki has an uncanny ability to attract disaster and chaos in the most banal of everyday situations, and has no need to fictionalise her catalogue of embarassments.

Jo Manby is a 40-something ex-gallery girl and mother of one who writes for an academic race relations journal. Her degree is in English and French Literature and Art History and she has published art criticism extensively. In 2003 she won first prize in The Times / Hortus garden writing competition, and she is a practicing artist.

Annie Noble – I have come late in life to creative writing, having spent nearly thirty years working in cancer research. I am therefore very familiar with the rules and restrictions of scientific writing. In 2002 I embarked on the Creative Writing degree at Derby University and really enjoyed the freedom of writing "non-scientifically"! It has been great to make new friends and to stay in touch with them and The Uni Writers acts as a valuable spur to keep writing something! I love the ideas which come into my head and what happens when the writing process starts.

Nathanael Ravenlock discovered his passion for writing while volunteering in Australia. University provided him with three blissful years dedicated to the art. Now, although continuing to formulate new ideas, he rarely writes them down! His biggest influence, and distraction, is currently his son, who was born the day before Halloween in 2012.

Henryka Sawyer – born in Gniezno, Poland. Educated in Poland gaining a diploma in business studies. Resident in England for the past forty-one years. Widowed with one daughter, Aleks. I love reading, gardening, walking our dog Amber and lots of travel. Living in retirement with partner David. Encouraged to write by Peter Breheny, a friend for the past thirty years.

Denis Quigley – Clydebank born, graduated from Glasgow University with a degree in Computer Science. Worked for 25 years in software development in Liverpool, Glasgow and Dundee. Moved to Bermuda and took up general business consultancy for the next 10 years. In all that time, despite the claims about consultants, never wrote a single piece of fiction. Returned to semi retirement in the UK, eventually landing in Ashbourne, and took up writing short stories and painting very poor watercolours.

Frauke Uhlenbruch has been writing stories since the day she learned how to write. She grew up in Germany but has since lived in the U.S., Finland and the U.K. At the moment she is in the most fortunate position to be paid to write a PhD about utopia, science fiction, and the Bible at the University of Derby.

Harry Wilson – Born 1923 at Blaydon-on-Tyne, the youngest of nine children. As a school boy I always enjoyed composition, literature and drama. As a young man I joined 'The People's Theatre Newcastle,' where the theatrical experience laid the foundation for my interest in writing. Having written countless sketches, short stories, stage and radio plays over the years I was honoured to have one of my historical plays performed at Stafford Play House. During the war I served as an indentured engineering apprentice with Vickers-Armstrong. At the end of my apprenticeship I followed a career in sales eventually joining JCB in Staffordshire where in 1964 I was appointed sales director worldwide. Travelled the globe and clocking up more miles annually than the average airline pilot. On retirement I continued with my writing and mountaineering interests. Howay the laads!

***

Visiting – the theme of the book and this chapter emerged from the group as we progressed through the year and realised much of our work revolved around visits, visitors, and visiting.

100 Word Stories – the results of a group challenge to write a story using precisely one hundred words.

A Shooting Visit – inspiration from these pieces came from a visit to the Derby Rifle & Pistol Club 1999 where the group had a go at firing rifles and muskets.

Sculpture – stories following a visit to Simon Manby the sculptor.

Lowry – featuring work produced during a day trip to The Lowry in Salford.

Acknowledgements

Thanks to Jenny Ferry, the cake lady, for keeping us fed every month and expanding our waistlines. Thanks to Matt Black for writing the introduction, to narrator for typesetting the book and designing the cover, Annie Noble for the front cover photograph and to Jo Manby for proofreading.